FORGETTING ZOË

Also by Ray Robinson

Electricity
The Man Without

Ray Robinson

FORGETTING ZOË

WILLIAM HEINEMANN: LONDON

Published by William Heinemann 2010

2 4 6 8 10 9 7 5 3 1

First published in Great Britain in 2010 by
William Heinemann
Random House, 20 Vauxhall Bridge Road,
London SW1V 2SA

www.rbooks.co.uk

Addresses for companies within The Random House Group Limited can be found at:
www.randomhouse.co.uk/offices.htm

The Random House Group Limited Reg. No. 954009

A CIP catalogue record for this book
is available from the British Library

ISBN 9780434020324

The Random House Group Limited supports The Forest Stewardship
Council (FSC), the leading international forest certification organisation. All our
titles that are printed on Greenpeace approved FSC certified paper carry the FSC logo.
Our paper procurement policy can be found at: www.rbooks.co.uk/environment

Mixed Sources
Product group from well-managed
forests and other controlled sources
www.fsc.org Cert no. TT-COC-2139
© 1996 Forest Stewardship Council
FSC

Typeset in Fournier MT by Palimpsest Book Production Limited,
Grangemouth, Stirlingshire

Printed and bound in Great Britain by
CPI Mackays, Chatham ME5 8TD

This book is dedicated to
SARA MAITLAND

INSPIRED BY REAL EVENTS

At first glance there is little remarkable about Thurman Hayes. In this photograph, taken from his high school yearbook, he looks like an average teenager, with sandy hair and gray eyes and an amiable smile. The press interviewed local ranchers but no one said they had known Thurman or the Hayes family well, if at all. No one said that he was more or less a pleasant man, a nice man to talk to. No one said he was a harmless fellow who kept himself to himself. No one expressed any real surprise at what he'd done either . . .

April 19, 1995

Coyote Plains, Arizona

THURMAN STOOD next to Father on the veranda while the old man drank his breakfast glass of milk with raw egg. The sheet-metal sky seemed to have gone mad in its morning glare, but there were dirty clouds out there scudding the horizon.

Father scratched his weather-tanned neck. His grin was a challenge.

'Sure you wouldn't rather be at school, doing algebra and kissing the girls?'

Thurman was almost fifteen years old and claimed to have an upset stomach. Father said that if he was staying at home then he had to help him out on the ranch, you choose.

When Father looked into the rhyme of Thurman's face it was obvious he hated what he saw: his own weaknesses, his failings. No matter how often he took the belt or the boot to the boy, he couldn't toughen him up. You should have been a fucking girl. Often he told Thurman this.

'Looks like it'll rain, sir.'

'Mayhaps it will, mayhaps it won't.'

They headed out into the morning light, Thurman watching Father out the corner of his eye, how the old man was beginning to stoop.

It was midday before Mom found them. She approached on horseback as they paused. The horse stamped, snorted, scissoring its ears. Father broke her in, Thurman thought, just like he broke that horse.

'It's Oklahoma,' she said.

'Oklahoma what?'

'You gotta come see.'

'We ain't . . .'

'Eugene, there's been a bomb.'

Father spent the rest of the day glued to the television set, watching the replicated images of the collapsed Federal Building and rescue workers pulling bodies from the rubble. The following morning Thurman asked where he was.

Mom raised her eyebrows. 'Guess.'

She always observed in silence, feigning aloofness, treading around Father while he thought his thoughts, a man who detested being watched or misunderstood for even a second and who seemed eternally confused by the mystery of living in his own skin. He was a glass-is-half-empty man, an ornery piss-vinegar never-quit. He came from a family of hard-scrabble cattle ranchers, ancestry flowing back through Texas, Tennessee, the Cumberland Gap and West Virginia. His family rode in the Texas 2nd Cavalry during the Civil War and fought in the Battle of the Bulge and he was quick to let you know about it.

For the two weeks following the Oklahoma bombing, Father hid away down in the bunker. The entrance was situated behind a concealed doorway in the garage, accessible from the rear of the house and also the kitchen. This doorway opened onto stairs that led down through three sets of doors, leading to a fourth, 300-pound steel door that once belonged on a bank vault, fitted back in the late 1950s. The bunker was 110 inches long, 72 inches wide and 230 inches from floor to ceiling. The walls consisted of an outer shell of fourteen-inch and an inner shell of sixteen-inch reinforced concrete, creating an anechoic, soundproof chamber.

During those two weeks Father set about turning the bunker into a habitable space, making plans to install a new ventilation system, toilet and washbasin, some recessed lighting and a stockpile of bottled water and potassium iodide, treatment for radiation sickness.

One day he gripped Thurman by the shoulders. 'Because the fireball vaporizes all matter and matter absorbs neutrons,' he said. 'Because it kicks out beta particles and gamma rays and you got to be prepared, you never know. Twenty:twenty hindsight is useless when you're shitting your internal organs out.' Moist-eyed, he'd rant about President Truman and the Alert America campaign. He even bemoaned the Cuban Missile Crisis as a lost opportunity. Now father and son were using the bunker for the same reason and that reason had nothing to do with doomsday obsessions.

Thurman found Father's stash of girly magazines hidden at the bottom of a cardboard box, beneath newspaper clippings about the bombing. The magazines were in pristine condition, almost as if they had never been looked at, and Thurman was careful not to crease them and always wiped his fingerprints off afterwards. But no matter how long he stared at the images, he failed to feel a thing.

1999

Four years later

THE SLAM of the front door; the sound of Father's pickup revving; tires churning through the dirt. Only recently had Thurman stopped running down to the bunker when his parents went on like this. Nineteen now, too old for hidey-holes.

He walked through the house towards Mom's bedroom, wading through the quiet Father's absence shaped.

She was lying in the dark. He stepped towards the bed.

'Mom?'

'For mercy sake, Thurman.'

And so he echoed Father's flight, slamming the screen door behind him, stomping down the veranda steps and revving the old, oil-guzzling jalopy.

As the track bent due north he could see the wink of Father's brake lights in the distance, two red squares burning then departing beyond the high ridge of the mesa. He rubbed his eyes. The evening heat made him unctuous and snarky. He peeled his shirt from his back and cranked down the window. Forty minutes later he was driving through the town along the length of the main thoroughfare, out past the bars and down by the railroad tracks.

It was here that he slowed to a crawl, one finger on the steering wheel. Father's Dodge pickup with its repair spots and creased fender, the tarp and orange ropes rolled up on the bed, was parked behind a station wagon. The jalopy engine puttered through Thurman's thighs as he watched the light flicker above the doorway. Everyone knew it was the brothel. Father's weekly toot. Thurman imagined an ageing woman, ugly and painted. Father's rawboned shoulders sloping above her.

The grooves of the steering wheel bit into his palm.

Often Father would return home drunk and incensed from these weekly trips, and Thurman would run to his room and crouch on the floor, thighs pressed against his chest, praying in his dread-filled way for them to stop, for it to stop, trying to remember a time when things were different, but there never was such a time. He would hear the sound of Mom's blouse buttons hitting the wooden floor and knew that soon he would have to go to her room and hold her. Sometimes she appeared to be hallucinating with pain but never once did she cuss Father. Never hid. Never argued. Never fought back. She must have learned way before Thurman was born that life was easier if she remained mute. Slut. Whore. Thurman would lie in the dark picturing her biting her lips, moaning the moan of a good wife because she knew that if she uttered a wrong word Father would drop his fist onto her face. Cunt.

When he thought about Father it was always the old man's hands he saw in his mind, whopping great shovels, always active, either out on the ranch or at home, nothing Father could not make nor fix. Long-fingered and gnarled, his hands were so expressive that he tended to talk with them and at times he appeared conscious of this and would tuck them into his pockets or sit on them. Father's hands even moved, Mom said, when he was asleep. But to Thurman the hands only ever spoke one word and that word was hurt. They contained bones that had fractured many times and reset, broken against walls and furniture, the skulls of cattle, Mom, Thurman. Hands so masterful at gripping axes and shovels and carpentry tools and soldering irons, the stock of his rifle and shotgun. So useful for overturning a table with a single, effortless flick, for giving backhand so fast it was heard before it was felt, for grabbing a fistful of hair and smashing heads into walls.

In comparison Thurman's hands were clumsy, with square-tipped sausage fingers. He was the exact opposite of a punk kid and Father would often take him angrily to task for having failed to fight back, for being mouse-like, meek. He didn't understand what was going on inside Thurman's skull. Didn't sense the nest of neuroses being knitted into more and more complex patterns each and every day.

As a form of punishment Father would press one of his hands down on top of Thurman's head so forcefully that Thurman's legs would buckle, and then he would dig his bone-hard nails into Thurman's scalp, drag them back and forth so deep that blood would trickle down his forehead and swim in his eyes and God help him if he flinched. I've more strength in my little finger, Father would say.

Thurman put the pickup into gear and drove towards the highway.

He stopped to buy some cigarettes. The place looked deserted. He walked across the gravel lot, puddles of oil reflecting the red neon sign of the Southern Skies Motor Hotel. The man behind reception was a deaf-mute who gasped and blinked while serving him. Behind the man a steer's head was mounted on the wall, watching them both with dusty eyes.

Thurman nodded, 'Thank you, sir,' and the man made an oblique gesture with his fingers.

Outside, a young woman was leaning against a trashcan.

'Mind if I mooch a cigarette, mister?'

Thurman scanned her: russet-colored Naugahyde jacket, unzipped; clingy white blouse; no hose; maybe four-foot-eight in her bare feet. He removed the plastic wrapper from the Lucky Strike pack and passed her one.

She winked. 'Light my fire?'

As she leaned towards the flame he noted the smudges under her eyes and scabs around her mouth and the split in her lower lip.

She stared towards the road blowing out smoke as if Thurman wasn't there.

Distant sound of traffic laying rubber along the highway.

Insects whirring like maracas in the dark.

'You staying here?'

She took a long time to look at him. Blinked once.

He asked, 'You need a ride?'

He drove due north. He was a steady, tenacious driver who disliked changing lanes or passing because driving made him minutely conscious of himself. It was a Sunday night, near midnight, and the highway was quiet. He noticed her smell, a cheap-smelling perfume more animal than floral. Headlights reflecting off the blacktop illuminated them both.

He sneaked looks at her. The girl was a train wreck but almost pretty. She sat sucking and blowing blue-white smoke, clacking her mouth, bare feet up on the dashboard showing her badly painted, cherry-colored toenails.

She mashed a butt and then reached for the Lucky Strikes.

'Help yourself,' he said, trying to be funny.

She asked, 'Got any gum?'

'No.'

'Beer?'

'Nope.'

'Weed?'

'Sorry.'

She made a face. 'Don't be.'

He'd told her he was driving to the next town, a clear twenty miles through the desert, nothing but tumbleweed and darkness between. He wondered did the man on the motel reception see her climb into the jalopy. Deaf-mute, Thurman thought. Man ain't blind.

'So where you from, sounds Midwestern?'

When she didn't answer he looked over at her and she shrugged.

'And how old are you?'

'How old I look?'

He watched the speedometer. 'Same age as me, I guess. Nineteen?'

She laughed briefly. 'Yeah. That's right, mister. I'm nineteen.'

A girl with no suitcase, no possessions, no shoes. She placed her big toe against the dial on the radio and twisted. He looked at her and smiled and she smiled back, putting pictures in his head he knew weren't right.

'Won't get reception out here,' he said. 'There's cassettes under yon seat.'

'Anyone ever told you ya talk funny?'

He didn't trust his voice to respond. His old-timer mannerisms and way of speaking. You get raised by old folk and this is how you act.

She bent down, causing her blouse to open a little. He looked. Breast buds. Bulge of nipples like swollen-shut eyes, peeping out at him. He leaned towards the wheel.

'Johnny Cash. Townes Van Zandt. Willie Nelson. You for real?'

She slid a cassette in, then reached for the lighter on the dashboard.

He wondered could she sense it.

A road sign full of bullet holes said the town was three miles.

. He cleared his throat and told her how he'd wanted to study electrical engineering after high school but Father wouldn't let him. 'I wish Mom would tell me we were leaving. To drive away and never return.'

The girl rubbed her feet. 'Mm-hmm,' she said.

He wondered what it would be like to spend a night with her, the girl in her panties in a cigarette-stale motel room, passing trucks striping their bodies with headlights through the curtains.

He couldn't see anything in his rearview mirror; not the red neon jewel of the Motor Hotel; no hint, even, of the dividing line between land and sky; just the dim smolder of his tail lights. Maybe this could be a new beginning. Leave the ranch behind and just keep on driving. He stared at her, daring her to interpret the look in his eyes. He took his foot off the accelerator and steered onto the gravel berm but she didn't appear to notice. He dropped the pickup down a gear and she looked at him curiously, defiantly. He steered back into the road, thinking about the gun hidden under the back seat.

He pulled up outside the old town jail. The atmosphere felt taut.

'Well, thanks for the ride,' she said.

He opened his mouth, gripping the steering wheel as the door slammed shut and her silhouette snaked along an alleyway to Johnny Cash singing 'Streets of Laredo'.

He exhaled. He'd wanted to ask, You got some money? A place to stay? I'll look after you, he'd wanted to say.

He placed his hand over the warm vinyl where she'd been sitting and brought his sweaty palm to his nose. Their mingled smells.

He put the jalopy into gear and cruised the deserted streets.

MOM WAS in her nightgown with curlers in her hair. She plumped her pillows and patted the space beside her. 'Come on.'

Thurman sat next to her for an hour, watching TV without a word passing between them, the color of the screen bathing their faces. When the show finished she picked up the remote, turned the volume down and switched on her lamp, asking Thurman if he was OK.

'Why?'

'I'm your mother, Thurmy. It's my job to worry.'

'I'm fine, ma'am.'

She raised her brows at him, patting her breastbone with her fingertips. Faint, hollow taps. 'I wanted more children, you know.'

'Where'd that come from?'

'Thought I was too old for hatching babies. Eugene was so angry with me, like it was my fault. But I never asked him to get checked. You know?'

Thurman nodded.

'I'd given up wishing a long time before you made an appearance. Eugene accused me of sleeping with another man.'

'Jesus.'

She aped Eugene's voice: 'Marny, who's the goddamn father?'

They laughed at her rendition.

'I was forty-four. Thought I was going through the change.'

He didn't want to hear it. 'I know,' he said.

'That's when he moved downstairs to his little room. The Sulking Room, I called it. Soon as he saw you, he knew. Two peas in a pod.'

'Mom.'

She tapped the back of his hand. 'Don't pull that face. It's true, whether you like it or not.'

'But I'm not *like* him.'

After a moment she said quietly, 'When I look at you, son, my cup runneth over. Truly it does.'

She stroked his knuckles and he became aware of the blood coursing through his veins. Unbidden he recalled the particular sound of fabric swishing against skin and the crackle of static electricity as Mom pulled her nightdress over her hair.

'I've never liked it here,' she said. 'I almost left after the first year. Stuff you know nothing of. Eugene bought me a rifle for our first wedding anniversary and I thought: well, that says it all.' Thurman listened to the relic sing-song quality of her voice, how it had been bleached and trampled smooth by the desert, but still the old dialect would slip through like chinks of light. Often she would mutter a phrase to herself, staring inwardly, northwards. 'I missed Canada. My friends. That's the trouble with this place; you don't get to know anyone. Not really. Too much space between things. I never got to know any of the local women.' She elbowed him playfully. 'Or the men. But the amount of times I've begged him to take me back, on vacation, anywhere. But the ranch. Always Coyote Plains this, Coyote Plains that.'

Thurman opened his mouth, hesitated.

'I'd like a grandchild afore I die,' she said.

He climbed from the bed and walked over to the window, leaning his forehead against the cool glass.

'I met someone,' he said.

Silence flexed behind him.

'When?'

'You don't know her. She's not from around here.'

'When will I meet her?' A shade to her voice. 'I'd like to meet this girl.'

Thurman turned to her. 'Would you like me to make some supper?'

'Tsk. It's too late for supper.'

'You're hungry though?'

'I'm fine.'

'Your stomach's been snarling the past hour.'

'But Eugene . . .'

'Father won't hear. I'll be super-quiet.'

She had a way of looking at him at times, a look of collusion that filled his head with goofy notions. He was always reading messages that weren't there.

'Just some toast,' she said. 'With jam.'

'Apricot?'

She nodded. 'And then you can tell me more about this girl.'

HE GOT duded up. He put on his pastel-blue stag-cut shirt with the floral print motif across the chest that Mom said *became* him. He liked the sound of it: becoming Thurman. Liked the way the shirt showed off his solid, tanned arms. Father said he looked like a fag in it, but what the fuck did he know.

Father's room was empty and so he quickly used Father's cologne and dashed out of the house. On the veranda a sound ensnared him. He tilted his head, waited; Mom's sounds, Father's sounds. Going at each other again. He climbed into the old jalopy and drove away, cussing as he steered through the cholla and mesquite.

He'd score some marijuana from a guy he knew from high school – the guy's name was Carl, a dropout who joined the Marine Corps at seventeen but was forced to leave and was now, if gossip was correct, a professional stoner. Then Thurman would drive across the desert to the next town and search the bars for the barefoot girl. He pictured them smoking weed together, her face illuminated by the dashboard lights.

Thurman didn't like to think about high school because

he always remembered going on that single, sorry-ass date with a girl in his grade called Anna – a studious girl with a startled-looking, almost beautiful face and sticky-out ears. Thurman thought he was so cool because they had a reservation for dinner, but he hadn't got a license yet and so Mom had to drive them to the restaurant. Thurman wore one of Father's old suits and Anna wore a blue velvet dress. She blushed when he gave her the pink corsage that Mom had bought him. 'Golly Moses,' was her response. After dinner Mom drove them to the school dance and they had their picture taken against a fake Parisian backdrop. Later he gave Anna the love letter he wrote. For an evening, at least, Thurman felt like one of the other kids.

But that date amounted to diddly. Never was there a second date. Never did he get to give Anna his name bracelet. Never did they sit next to each other at lunch or walk along the field holding hands. He knew his love letter had been circulating around school but no one said a word to him directly and that was the worst part. A year later everyone in his grade got their licenses and started driving up the loop to Mount Misery and he'd hear about the booze and camping and sex binges going on. Some of the girls got pregnant before graduating; Anna was one of those girls.

Thurman drove down past the stockyards and pulled up outside Carl's old house. A low-slung tow-truck in the driveway. A swing chair on the rickety porch. A single light glowing in an upstairs window.

The basement was a dark clutter, air fetid with damp and the tang of urine. It was some kind of lab. Carl stood for a few seconds running his hands through his lank hair, jiggling his legs. He looked white-trash hillbilly in his raggedy slacks and oversized shirt, and those whiskers on his face were just plain dumb.

'Need to get this shit spick and span,' he said.

Thurman took in every detail: bottles of brick and driveway cleaner on wooden table tops; cans of starting fluid; empty K-Mart bags; piles of Vicks inhalers and eyedroppers and small glass bottles; bowls and coffee filters; baking dishes and test tubes; rubber gloves and cotton balls. In the corner of the room a motorbike frame sat on an oil-stained rug surrounded by engine parts.

'Who's this pissant?'

The voice scared Thurman silly.

A man walked into the light coming from the single bulb. He was six feet tall with a blue-lipped, emaciated face peering from beneath a felt fedora. He reminded Thurman of a Nazi.

Thurman reached for his cigarettes.

'Don't spark that up in here,' Carl said. 'He's just an old schoolfriend, Lex. Come to score some blow.'

Thurman offered his hand but the old man went back to his seat. 'The name's Lexington,' he rasped. 'As in Lexington Avenue. Where I was conceived.'

'During the Civil War,' Carl said.

'Fuck you, peckerwood.'

'My gramps, in case you're wondering.'

'Pleased to meet you.'

'Back at ya,' Lex said. 'We just got us a fresh batch cooked. What's your family name, son?'

'Hayes.'

'Hmm. So you're Eugene's kid? That's one triple-mean-assed sonofabitch.'

Thurman snorted. 'Yep.'

'And you a chip off the old block, I guess?'

'No, sir.'

Lex leaned back into shadow. 'Eugene never done my family no dirt, but I wouldn't want to cross that ornery bastard. He's a bit bubble off plumb, you dig?'

Thurman noticed an empty holster hanging from Lex's chair arm.

'Queers call it 'tina. As in Christina,' Lex added.

Carl carried something over to the old man. A sniff, a breathy sigh. Then Carl approached Thurman with the circular hand mirror and a plastic tube.

Carl's eyes stared inward.

Thurman asked, 'What's in it?'

'Crank. Cut with Mannitol.' Lex's voice sounded delicate, wispy. 'Real smooth. Make your dick stand on end.'

Thurman inspected the two lines of white crystalline powder. 'I don't know.'

'Take the fat one. The rock star one.'

'When I said dope I meant weed,' Thurman said. 'Marijuana.'

Carl looked vexed. 'Trust the crank, it'll put hair on your lemons. Here.'

Thurman took the mirror.

Carl began scratching his forearms. 'Crank tics. Fuck.'

'I'll bet my swollen left testicle he won't.'

Such foulness scorched his blood and scoured his synapses, peppered and spiced. The fire in his nasal cavity licked the flipside of his eyeballs and as he wept he couldn't stop laughing. If he could see more he might go blind; hear more he might go deaf. He had to bite his thumb-knuckle to stop his jaw from grinding. Lex was slow-nodding, on a different beat. Carl sat hunched in the corner chatting to his motor-bike, praying to his machine. He had assembled the engine and fitted it and now he was disassembling it again.

'How you feeling, sonny? Peppy?'

'Choice. Real choice.'

'Ain't everything just so bright and shiny and happy?'

Thurman's heart hammered so hard his eyes kept swarfing.

Lex was handling a shiny pistol, a small, hefty-looking, .38 Lady Derringer. The old man cocked and uncocked the hammer, quicker each turn.

Thurman asked, 'Where's the john?'

'Up the stairs, take a right.'

With each step up his eyes faded. He stopped outside the john door then kept on walking. The night outside was a bare-knuckle punch to his senses. He spotted some bushes behind a wind-rattled shed and dropped his pants and emptied the diarrhea, Mom's screams running amuck inside him.

HE DROVE across the desert, beers clinking on the back seat. There was a real mess of a rainstorm that night, a colossal front had been gathering on the horizon for days like a killer wave, moving inwards so slow the eyes couldn't perceive. Finally it was upon them and Thurman had pitched and rolled in his bed like he was fighting a rip tide, awake into the small hours, the shoeless hitchhiker harassing his thoughts.

He had just spent the last four days in bed feeling sandbagged, like the bottom had fallen out of his life. All he could remember was Lex playing with his Lady Derringer and then waking up in the bunker with Father kicking him. 'I heard what went on last night,' Father said. 'Gone to a bar and got beaten? You let those men *hurt* you? Crazy as a shithouse rat.'

And Mom, as per, pretended nothing had happened.

Rain slicked the windscreen as Thurman eyed the speedometer, wondering about the pressure in the tires. He passed a station wagon parked on the shoulder but thought nothing of it, then a few hundred meters down the road he saw a figure walking stooped against the rain.

He pulled over, waited. Cranked down the window.
His blood bloomed.
'You need a ride, ma'am?'

THURMAN FOUND Father asleep on a mattress on the bunker floor, wearing nothing but his stained union suit. The vinegar reek of his feet.

'Sir?'

Father laid his scowl on Thurman, blinking lapis-blue eyes. 'What?'

'You sure you're OK?'

'Eh?'

'Why don't you let me help you? You know I'm handy. Know I'm good with electronics and stuff.'

Father picked his ruby-veined nose. 'I know you talk like a goddamn girl.'

'We both knows you been doing things wrong.'

'And I know I despise everything you is. Now do the fuck you're told. Get.'

Thurman stared back, unyielding in the moment.

'Yessir.'

The following morning Thurman drove out to the mailbox to await the package of Restoril he'd ordered off the Internet. He raised his binoculars and glassed the vehicle raising dust at the edge of the property. Removing his Stetson, he rubbed sweat from the back of his neck and forehead. The sky was down on its hunkers, baring its teeth, cacti shadows thrown wildly across the track.

The mailman stepped out of his vehicle and passed Thurman the box addressed to Mr Eugene Hayes. The mailman tried to make small talk as Thurman signed the form and walked away.

He put the pickup into gear and stared at his shaking hands. 'Stop.' He clenched and unclenched them. 'Stop.' They didn't stop.

Part way home Mom drove past him on her way into town, sounding her horn and waving through the windshield, and when he parked in front of the house he realized he was still smiling at her.

The garage door was open, the jalopy parked inside.

Thurman went up to his room and hid the parcel under his bed and came back down to the garage calling, 'Sir? Hello?'

Just the breathy sound of the ventilator pulling air down into the bunker.

He walked over to the door that stood ajar and eyed the steps down there. He held his breath to listen: the faint squawk of the radio and a tap-tapping noise, Father's old-timer cologne hanging on the air.

He looked over at the jalopy, its tail pipe next to the griddle of the ventilation shaft. It had been four years since the Oklahoma bombing, since Father started his renovations, and he'd told Father more than once that the controls for the ventilator should be down in the bunker, not above. They both knew Thurman was right but the pigheaded old bastard wouldn't listen.

The mean inside Thurman bubbled to a boil.

He climbed into the jalopy, turned the key and pressed the gas. The engine stumbled, puttered. The gas gauge said it was almost empty. He hoped there'd be enough. He waited, listened. No response from the bunker below.

He closed the garage door. Already the pungent monoxide stench was into his bloodstream and to the brain, making him reel. He made his descent, adrenalin searing his veins, the narrow passageway body-hugging, and Father's shadow jumped as he reached the final step.

Slamming the steel door shut, leaning his shoulders against it, he heaved his full might backwards, hermetically sealing the bunker, creating a gas chamber. His boot heels found purchase along the second and third risers as he pushed with all his strength. The door handle kept on turning, turning. His rasp and suck through gritted teeth, as if Thurman himself were choking. Between these breaths came the faint sound of Father's shouts, the percussion of his fists slamming the other side of the door. The two men pitting against each other.

Thurman hung almost horizontal, his body shaking, leg muscles spasming. A high keening came from his lips. How long would it take? He kept on pushing, imagining Father covering his face, flailing his arms about like that may save him.

'Ain't afraid of you *none*,' Thurman screamed. 'NONE.'

Faint but distinct, he heard the sound of Father's laughter. Between chokes and coughs, Father was laughing into death's noxious breath, 'Ha. Ha. Ha. Ha.' Staccato like gunshots, hastening the asphyxiation. This handful of minutes seemed to last for ever, but soon there came an insect-like tapping, and Thurman pictured Father lying on the other side of the door, convulsing in some epileptic final throe, bleeding from the mouth.

Silence.

Thurman slumped forward, hands on thighs. He arched his back and kicked the cramp from his legs and pressed his ear against the cold steel. Nothing. He put his hand on the door handle. Paused.

He climbed up into the garage and hit the daylight running, inhaling like a newborn. The gas in the jalopy would run out soon, the engine die. He shut the door behind him and climbed into the flatbed and looked briefly at the house in the side mirror before steering away, cutting across the land towards the town where he would sit in the movie theater chewing popcorn and sucking root beer through a straw.

LISTENING TO Mom move through the rooms of the house, as if she expected to find Father hiding someplace. She said she didn't know what to do or who to call. The engine had stopped some time ago but still the fumes were unbearable. She'd gone down there hollering and opened the door and found Father lying on the floor and rushed back up the stairs and sat on the veranda waiting as the sky bowed through to dusk, until she saw Thurman's headlights striping the land. At the edge of Mom's voice he was certain he heard relief. He called the coroner and when the man re-emerged he said it looked like Father had changed his mind and tried to escape but had somehow locked himself in. He'd seen it before. Suicide. Common in these parts.

'I'll make sure the sheriff is satisfied. No need to trouble you folks no more. And I'll contact the undertaker for you.'

Once the coroner had left Mom turned to Thurman and said, 'You're the man of the house now.' When Mom said these words, Thurman thought of two things. Whenever she bossed him about he would always imagine shouting back at her, about how, one day, it would be him barking the orders in this house. But of course he never did. Then he remembered how Father would sometimes call Mom 'Mother', and how sticky it made him feel.

Dust storms were reported to be blowing in from the east, but the morning was still and unusually cold. The cortège was small, all-male, neighboring ranchers and men from the town Father used to play cards with. The priest looked half asleep. The men shook Mom's hand and muttered a few words. When the priest finished she invited them into the house and they stood in the parlor talking quietly in pairs, drinking whiskey. As they left they offered their assistance. 'The lad won't cope,' they told her. Thurman had just turned nineteen.

He got up as usual the following day and had a light breakfast and went outside. Mom called to him from the shade of the veranda. 'Forget it,' she said. She phoned one of the men and a team of vaqueros arrived and within a couple of days the land was empty of livestock. She had gates built across the grids and put up signs. VIOLATORS WILL BE PROSECUTED. THAT MEANS YOU.

One morning he watched her remove the pinions from her hair and throw them in the trash. She began going into town a lot, and in the evenings the house was full of music and laughter. They would watch TV or look at old photographs; his favorite was the one of her taken when she was a little girl, back on the island in northern Canada, sat on the harbor wall wearing a short skirt and with dirty knees. She is looking to one side, distantly; as if she knew her adult life would be led far away from here. He wished he could have known her back then, and that they had grown up together. Thinking how he had never seen the ocean. How terrifying it must be.

She wouldn't tell him how she ended up in Arizona with Father 4,000 miles south. She muttered something about an aunt in Phoenix, about a dance, like it pained her too much to think about it. 'My life took a wrong turn,' was all she'd say. 'No U-turn. Putting down roots in this dust that's good for nothing.'

It was late summer, lightning season in the desert. Dust storms had been whipping up static charge and the lightning took on a new energy that year, pulling light from the sky, leaving Thurman red-eyed and sniffling. Electricity presaging the August rains, those blood-red floods. Mom would sit on the veranda in her rocking chair, smoking and drinking, the surrounding brush and cacti glowing with electrical charge. Thurman used to be terrified of the storms as a child because he believed the entire earth was about to be consumed with dust. Father once told him, 'One day everything will be covered, all the cities and highways, all life, and the Papagos will roam as they once did.'

So this was Mom in mourning, buying antiques and going to the betting shop in town, four, five times a week. He'd thought Father's death would bring them closer.

'Why don't you go traveling? Go visit relatives?'

'Chance would be a fine thing. I cut myself off from them years ago. They won't want to see me after so long. And Eugene hated his side of the family. No.'

'We'll go back to the island, like you always said you wanted to. I went and applied for a passport in town.'

She gave off a moan that smeared her face. 'I don't want

to see the change of the place,' she said. 'And I don't want the place to see the change in me.'

That look in her eye; it reminded him of the pain as she beat him as a child. The pain was like an insect clicking at the edge of his memories.

'When we first got married, your father used to ask me to piss on him.'

Thurman blinked, recalling the night she caught him masturbating in the bathtub, in the water she'd just climbed from. 'Playing with your uglies in my filth!' she screamed, returning with the horsewhip.

'He would follow me into the bathroom. Thought it was intimate. Because it came from me it was something like a gift.'

'You're funning with me?'

'And you know, I think the most intimate thing he ever did for me was scratch my back in bed at night. *Claw me back . . .*'

'You telling me you miss him?'

Father's final, staccato laugh, jouncing around his skull.

'We all suffer at the hands of those we love, Thurman.'

He decided Father's bedroom was his territory now. He swiped everything on Father's desk onto the floor and set his computer there, and then he gathered all of Father's belongings and fired up the brick incinerator out behind the cattle shed and burned the lot.

Mom's company was beginning to trouble him, he was certain she knew that Father's death was no suicide. He started to think a lot about the young women, the hitch-hikers he'd had in his flatbed, riding shotgun as he cruised the highways over the summer. The smell of them. The sound of their voices telling their stories. The intimacy of their body heat beside him.

He found himself driving to his old junior school with no intention other than to watch the children leave, or so he tried to convince himself. But one day, after all the children had gone, a small girl, maybe six or seven years old, was left waiting at the gates alone. The girl looked a little bit like Mom when she was younger, same biscuit-blonde hair and pale northern skin. She needed caring for.

The surprising feeling of his hardness; so commanding, authoritative.

'I told you,' he said in Father's voice. 'I ain't done yet . . .'

But he was done and it disgusted him. He wiped his fat fingers on his jeans.

He looked up: the girl was staring at him as if she sensed what he had just done to himself. She picked up her school bag and walked towards the flatbed and everything inside Thurman collapsed. But when he looked up again she had gone.

Two months Mom lasted without Father. Soon after they buried Father, Thurman discovered Mom was dying and had been for some time. She kept her trips to the hospital a secret but now she was refusing treatment and decided it was the right time to tell him. She knew he couldn't handle it. That's what she told him.

'Handle what? The fact that you're a liar?'

'Don't say that. Please. It hurts me to hear you say that.'

He saw the cancer inside her, yellow bloom feeding off her organs.

'So all the gambling you been doing? To rob me of Father's money before you die, that it?' He shot a glance over to the window and sensed the limits of the land outside, his inheritance of dust. He waggled his fingers in her face. 'Fritter fritter fritter.'

She turned away. 'I know you're . . .'

He grabbed her nightdress around the neck and the first slap brought a silence to the room, his handprint making her look like she was blushing. The final slap became a fist and when he saw the blood bubbling from her nose he ran and hid himself down in the bunker.

The next day she acted like nothing had happened, like the last thing she wanted for him to say was I shouldn't ought to have done that, forgive me.

He despised her in a way that became comfortable and he hated himself for it. Hated the fact that she was dying; that soon he would be truly alone in the world and he couldn't tell her how much he needed her. And he hated the fact he would never forget how it felt, as a small boy, being beaten by this woman.

In the world of Thurman and Mom, it had simply gone beyond that.

THE GIRL was stood in exactly the same position beneath the red neon glow of the Southern Skies Motor Hotel, leaning against a trashcan, one leg raised. Thurman cranked the window down, smiled. Chewing gum, she tilted her head to one side and squinched her eyes, and then she sashayed her fanny on over, white high-heels scraping the gravel of the apron.

He lowered the pitch of his voice, 'Need a ride?'

'You read my mind, mister.' She climbed into the passenger seat, filling the cab with the delicious scent of cinnamon gum.

He searched the walls, the rooflines of the rundown motel for security cameras. Nothing. He put the flatbed into gear and hit the blacktop.

'You make a habit of this?'

'What?'

'Getting lifts from strangers.'

'You ain't no stranger. Besides, I'm used to getting around with my thumb.'

Thurman held out his hand. 'My name's . . .'

'Ask your name, did I?' She unzipped her Naugahyde

jacket and shuffled about in her seat. 'Ask no questions and I'll tell no lies,' she said, punctuating the sentence with a pop of gum.

'I'd be obliged if you spat that out, missy. Right now.'

Her eyes widened. 'Well *excuse* me.'

The sound of her fingers being sucked made his mouth water. He watched the white lines passing beneath the flatbed and they were arrows of lust flying into him.

'Your family from here, then?'

She rearranged her legs. 'Me and my pappy, we never did talk. I mean I talked. Course I did. He just don't listen. Deaf-mute.'

'The guy who runs the motel?'

'Ten out of ten, Sherlock. But no, that man's my uncle. They twins. Both deaf-mute. Genetic. Too many of us be marrying into each other going way back. No, I'm from Idaho. Daddy sent me down here to straighten me out.'

The girl sniggered; Thurman sniggered. She glared.

'Don't he ought to care for you himself?'

'Guess that's what's expected. But no, he's simple.'

He still hadn't asked her where she wanted to go. Knew there'd be no answer.

'Sorry.'

'Don't be. First sign of trouble and he ships me out here to Buttfuck, Arizona. Ain't seen him nigh on three, four year now.'

He shot her a glance: skinny pale neck, a neck that could've belonged to a woman thirty years her senior; hair hanging lank, the color of a dirty dishrag; and those lines around her mouth made her look like she'd spent her short life grimacing.

'You needed taking into hand, that it?'

'Bit light-fingered is all. Nothing major league.'

'How's it going?'

She removed her scuffed high-heels and put her feet up on the dash. Bare skin, no hose, wiggling toenails painted black. Slut.

'What *you* think. Got any burns?'

'Burns?'

She sighed. 'Cigarettes.'

'Under yon seat.'

He glanced sideways. Saw the laced hem of her brassiere.

'Can't see none.'

'Further under.'

The buttons of his fly bit him. He opened his legs, wanting her to see, but it went and died already. He leaned towards the wheel.

She lit up and he noticed the burls of warts along her knuckles, pale blooms. She shot him a glance. He eyed the road feeling the hot beads of her eyes, intelligent, but not too intelligent.

'Your boots, they ostrich?'

'Brand new. A present to myself after my father died.' Wanting to tell her: it were me who killed him.

'You got no old lady at home?'

It wasn't the response he wanted. 'My mom?'

'Wife, dumb ass. A sweetheart.'

Thurman stared down at the blacktop. I want to take you home.

'Nothing sexier than a cowboy with a gun. Two pistols. Chaps.'

'That right?'

'Yessiree. Enough to make a girl go crazy, seeing a man's eyes all dark under a hat brim. Nice butt in tight jeans. And those *heels*.'

'How old're you anyway?'

'Old enough to know I like cowboys.'

'And your mom?'

He looked at her, inviting her to look back, but the girl just stared out the side window blowing smoke.

'So you do this plenty? Get lifts around the place with men?'

'Uh-huh.'

'Been up in some trucker's camper shell? Up on his mattress like?'

'Could be I might say no to him. How'd you figure that?'

'You need looking after.'

'You offering, or're you just daffy in the head?'

'Watch that yap of yours. I may be liable to do something I'd regret.'

'You don't seem the sort to regret much.'

He barked a laugh. What a jackpot you're in.

'There's a bottle behind my seat. Catdaddy.'

As she reached behind him he tamped the brakes, pulled onto the berm and span the vehicle across the gravel median.

She opened the bottle in her lap. 'Thought we was going into town?'

Thurman rubbed his sweaty face.

'You heading the wrong way, mister.'

They rolled into the night, the land behind them lost.

'DON'T IT taste real pretty?'

They were down in the bunker, lying on a rug, one of Thurman's arms trapped beneath her neck. It was uncomfortable but he didn't move. He watched her as if she were still breathing and felt such inner peace, her lips so black in the candlelight. He'd used too much Restoril in the Catdaddy. You won't make the same mistake twice.

He whispered, 'Want us to rub our uglies together?'

For some reason he recalled the alley kitten he found in town when he was eight years old and how he managed to sneak it home beneath his coat while he rode the flatbed. He brought it down into the bunker and made it a nest but the next morning Father discovered them both and picked the kitten up by the scruff, holding it away from his body like vermin, and took it away. Days later Thurman found a gunnysack by the track; inside was the boot-flattened kitten, skull misshapen, fur stiff with blood, brain, scat. He pictured Father throwing the sack from the flatbed window as he drove into town, thinking nothing of it. Thurman buried the kitten in the desert marking the spot with a strange-shaped rock, but the next day he retraced his steps and was upset to find some animal had dug it up and carried it away. He'd brought his clasp knife. He wanted to cut it up, to see inside.

Leaning on his elbow, he pressed his mouth against the dead girl's lips, her breath icy, bitter. It excited him. He drew the air from her mouth like a cigarette, her chest making ticking noises. He leaned back, smiling, replaying the girl's final words, 'I don't like it thataway.' 'But I love you,' is what he said.

He took the lighter and lit her finger warts. The smell made him stop.

If only you hadn't gone and died. Could've kept you here.

He got to his feet and towered over her.

'Don't mind if I call you Anna, now, do you?'

MOM'S END came quick. She was propped up in bed wearing a babushka bandanna. She had grown so skinny over the past few weeks, maybe down to seventy pounds, and in places she looked almost translucent. She was becoming wraith-like and appeared aware of it, attempting to cover her body with bed sheets as if she were naked, trying to mask the sweet smell of death with the opened perfume bottles gathered along her bedside table.

'Did you find Eugene?' she asked, her voice the sound of paper rubbing against paper.

He shook his head.

'It's not how far you fall, son,' she said, 'it's the way you land.'

He cleared his throat, thinking about the previous night, driving the girl back here, the way she got quieter and quieter, the way it made him feel inside, her body turning to juice down there.

'You know what,' Mom said, 'those fairyduster blooms should be out by now. Be a good boy and go pick some for my table,' lifting a solitary finger as he left the room.

He stood in the yard for a minute watching a couple of

43

buzzards wheel on a thermal and a drifty, peaceful feeling came over him, the likes of which he hadn't experienced for such a long time. But all around him, he noticed, the cholla shadows, elongated and spectral, looked like petrified figures of human pain. He remembered hopping over them as a boy, lest he be hexed. He collected a small bunch of the blood-red flowers and when he returned he noticed how her room smelled of earth, of dust. He dropped the flowers onto the rug.

'What you go and do that for, Mom?'

Felt her earthly shadow pass through him.

IN THE midst of life we are in death . . .

Gobbledygook. Father, down there, beside Mom's shovel-hole, four feet to the left. Father in his wooden box. The two of them together again. Like Father could reach through the earth, like him and Mom ever held hands in this life. Thurman knew there'd be few today, that she hadn't touched many, just neighboring ranchers being polite and showing their respect, but their presence discomfited him. He knew what they said about him: that he was some kind of fairy. Faggot.

Of whom may we seek succor . . .

But that man there, dark stranger with the blood drained from him, head hangdog, wiping his face. He wouldn't meet Thurman's eyes.

But of thee, oh Lord, who for our sins are justly displeased . . .

Mom said to Thurman three days before she died: Eugene, he was missing pieces.

Thou knowest, Lord, the secrets of our hearts . . .

He hit the drink hard in them days. She clenched a fist and made a punching motion: I mean *hard*. Talking to himself. Nightmares. She said one time in the middle of winter he locked her in the cupboard in the shed, the one with the rat's nest. Can still remember the sound of the clasp being dragged, she said. She wet herself, screaming for him, but he didn't come. She was carrying Thurman inside her at the time. The noise the rats made. She vomited. Left her there all night, he did. Wishing she was gone, wanting out of life. Me and you, she said. Soon as I could. Back to Canada, to the island. Divorce the bastard. The shock of hearing her talk like this.

Shut not thy merciful ears to our prayer but us, Lord, most holy, oh God most mighty . . .

Mom. Father. The two of them dead. How life can change in a blink.

Oh holy and merciful Savior, thou most worthy judge eternal, suffer us not in our last hour . . .

She had the day all booked, and there was Father on the courthouse steps, begging her. Stay with me, for the lad's sake, if nothing else. She laughed at the time, telling Thurman all of this propped up on her pillows in her death-bed. No more fear inside. Must need my head looking at, she said. Called herself a dumb cow. The violence got dark. Mean. For a while Father seemed to take young Thurman under his wing, out by the old telephone trail showing him how to shoot downwind from prey, teaching him the names of local flora and fauna as if they held some kind of magic, repeating them like a mantra. Prickly pear. Beavertail. Night-blooming cereus. Mormon bush. But Thurman was more interested in injuring animals than killing them. Father said it was no way to act in the country, that the boy was happier taking an old radio set to pieces than being a man out on the land with a weapon.

Through any pains in death . . .

Father beating him because he wet the bed into his teens. It made the wetting worse, his lisp worse. Father's looming presence.

Tried it on, she said. Sneaking into her room at night. I just want some loving, he'd say. She let him on occasion because she wanted another young one. She were desperate. But he couldn't make it stand on end.

Like father like son.

To fall from thee . . .

The lowering began. Down into the dirt. All eyes watching Mom going down.

You want to know something? I wish I never met him. He was in pieces and I couldn't put him back together again and he took it out on me. I knew I should've had more, should've let him at me, kept the bed warm at night. Burying me first-born.

She looked at him blankly, blinked once. You never knew. You had a brother, Thurmy. Died young. William, he was called. After your grandpa. Father blamed himself. Hit the bottle. Was even more of a whelp themdays. And how I wished it was Eugene that was taken. Not William. Wished he could take William's place. I told myself this.

In the sure and certain hope of the resurrection to eternal life. Through Almighty God we commend our sister Marny Hayes and we commit her body to the ground . . .

Thurman stepped forward, fist in front of him towards the shovel-hole.

'Goodbye, Mom.'

Chin creased, he straightened his arm and opened his fist, the pitter-patter of soil spelling out his utter aloneness in the world, the consummate lull of her absence upon him with all its might.

Earth to earth, ashes to ashes, dust to dust . . .

'Mom.'

The Lord bless her and keep her . . .

Folk moving forward. Soil falling.

Be gracious unto her . . .

Earth.

Be gracious unto her . . .

Silencing her.

Gonna be so quiet now.

And give her peace . . .

Alone.

GREAT SADNESS was afoot in the world, trampling Thurman with size elevens. When he tried to recall the days following Mom's death he couldn't. Grief came in the form of confused inertia and what snapped him out of it was the telephone and how it kept on ringing. He would sit in the parlor and stare at it until it stopped. He thought it was the stranger who had stood beside Mom's grave, head hangdog. When the cortège left, Thurman got into his flatbed and followed the man's blue sedan, reading the man's bumper sticker over and over: *Evolution is Science Fiction*, wanting to ram the man off the road. He followed the sedan along the highway another mile before pulling over, laying his head against the wheel and filling the cab with his noise. Father, cuckolded by this God-fearing stranger. The rasp of Father's voice, 'All women are whores.'

Then Thurman got it into his head that if he answered the telephone it would be Mom on the other end, asking him why she was still here, in the ground beneath the tree. He began to worry that burying her was the wrong thing to do; that he had, in some way, affronted her even in death.

Mom had gone and she did not return, instead she stuck

in him like a thousand splinters, and with every blink or step, every humdrum daily movement, he was reminded of her absence. Slicing. Stabbing.

How can you talk?

How can you eat?

How can you breathe?

He considered leaving Coyote Plains and the whole of Arizona behind, because the silence, the claustrophobia of the vast landscape, was beginning to scare him. His voice bouncing off the walls began to sound unfamiliar, whining. The loneliness was violent. And then pretty soon he went and forgot what Mom's voice sounded like; all he could recall was the shape of her eyes as she laughed, the way they creased at the edges and the way those creases folded away the darkness inside of him.

Every morning he woke in her bed shouting, 'Yes, Mom,' blinking up at the ceiling, questioning whether it was true, thinking about the girl's body raising a stink down in the bunker. Burying his face in the pillow that still harbored Mom's scent, he heard the telephone trilling in his head.

Don't leave me here.

'Want I should take you back, Mom? That it?'

Finally he ran to the receiver, listened. Heard breathing.

'Mom?'

'Mr Hayes?'

'Yes?'

'We need you to come into the post office. Sign for your passport, sir.'

He'd forgotten all about it, the passport he'd ordered so that he and Mom could travel back up to Canada together. He listened to the dead tone for a long time before ripping the phone from the wall and smashing it into pieces on the veranda steps.

He walked over to the Palo Verde tree. The hump hadn't started to settle yet.

Something unnamable moved through him.

What a mess he'd made.

Diaphanous nets billowed in the window, flirting with the breeze, everything in the world was talking, conversing about him sleeping in Mom's bed. Father laughing.

The rain stopped.

He felt half-cocked. You need to be smart.

He waited until midnight and ran the extension cable from the house and hung a lamp in the Palo Verde tree and then heaved the machinery over there. The cloud-filled night overflowed with the sound of the ditch-witch digger hammering into the caliche, but he stopped at times to think of Father a few feet away and between his breaths came the distant crackle of the incinerator.

He removed his shirt and wiped the sweat from his muscles and splatted snot into the loam and roots. Then he began the shovel work. He enjoyed the burning strain on his muscles and told himself that this was man's work; it filled him with dumb pride. He rested and started again. The effort made him dizzy, his temples ached. He emptied the remaining water from the canteen into his half-blind, sweat-filled eyes. Eventually came the sound: the hollow thud of metal on wood.

You can turn back now. Fill it in. Walk away.

Don't leave me here.

He told the funeral home he didn't need a sealed casket,

that he wanted it to be as natural as possible. He wasn't thinking of this. He wasn't thinking at all. But he told them he wanted the cheapest and now he was so glad he did. He knew putrefaction would be under way and once the jig saw was through the lid the noxious odor told him so. He smeared the liniment across his top lip and cut the shape, leaving enough room around the shoulders for him to gain purchase. Eyes closed, he lifted the cut wood and heaved it above, climbing out the shovel-hole and falling silently through himself into the mound of damp earth, digging his fingers into it.

He looked. Was naught but her shell but something bit his soul.

Rictus of bared teeth. Fiendish smile.

He stared until he could focus no more, and then he smiled back at her.

He threw the ropes over the branches and climbed down. Holding his breath he lifted her, placing the rope around her shoulders, but when he felt the material of her green dress she entered his cells and moved through his bloodstream into his heart. He vomited against the wall of the shovel-hole, trying to catch it in his hands, to stop it from splashing her. Rubbed his fingers through his chest hair.

He clambered out and began his pulling on the rope and placed her body onto the rug. He dragged her over to the incinerator and positioned her on it. He stood for a long time watching the white smoke gyring away.

Then he filled Mom's coffin with the body of the girl.

'Little slut to keep you warm at night.'

At dawn he tamped the earth with his feet, jumping up and down on the dirt, screaming the scream of the wounded.

But the unearthed caliche was darker than the surrounding dirt and so he brushed over the mound with branches. In the tree above him a greasy raven cackled and guffawed.

He went back over to the incinerator where embers glowed beneath the body. Flesh hanging on bone, human-form. The pyre no way hot enough.

You should have known this.

With binoculars he glassed the land 360 degrees. It was as if the meaning of the word lay hidden there, as if he could read the landscape and secure some understanding from it, from the journey ahead into that nothingness. He dowsed the remains with a mixture of kerosene and benzene and then relit.

He unfolded Father's old maps across the floor and roughly traced the route he would take, working out approximate distances with pieces of paper along the scale legend, how long it would take to drive at an average of per hour, per day. Thinking he would collect his passport from town and maybe hire a van, but then he imagined the florescent lights of the border patrol, a fat man in a tan brown suit sitting in a booth asking what he was bringing into Canada while men with rifles searched the van. Too darn risky. He would have to think about this. He would have to be smart.

With a callused finger he traced his route through Arizona, New Mexico, Texas, Oklahoma, Missouri, Illinois, Indiana, Ohio, Pennsylvania, New York, New Hampshire and Portland, entering Canada at New Brunswick and driving on through Nova Scotia to catch the car ferry from Glace Bay Harbor.

He repeated the figure, rolled it around his mouth. Such

a prospect for someone who had never crossed the state line before. He whooped inside, looking over at the tin coffee box on the floor.

'I'm taking you home, Mom. Home.'

It was the end of September 1999. The past three months had created a twist in him from which there was no unraveling. In just over a week a young girl would be erased. Thurman's life as the man of the house was about to begin.

Unnr Island, Northern Canada

a few weeks before

Situated eight miles off the eastern coast of Newfoundland, the three ellipse-shaped islands of Unnr, Klibo and Stein huddle around the natural wharf of Drifa Flow like a burly, shielding arm. The islands were originally inhabited by Viking settlers in AD 986 during their search for new lands in the western Atlantic, and the Norse culture and Norn dialect are still evident today. The largest town on the island of Unnr is Gulber Voe, overshadowed by the surrounding hills of Asgard Fea . . .

ZOË HEADED up into the hills, stopping at times to peer into the sky as warm rain fizzled past her, lifting her face to it. She wasn't like other children, weather-shy. Summer days praying for the rain to end? Tired of staring through rain-splattered windows? No. She would be out there among it, singing, soaked through. She was a true Canadian girl of big sky, big moon, of big sunsets and clouds.

Einar was sat on a bench staring out to sea. 'Whadd'ya at, boy?'

She perched beside him. 'I'm a girl, silly.'

A swap of wind slapped her cheeks; hollers of sea music came from below.

He touched her hair and said something she didn't catch. Einar, his checkered tam-o'-shanter at a jaunty tilt, his furze of beard and thicket of brows and eyes checking her over until she frowned. He'd been friends with Ingrid, Zoë's mother, for a couple of years now, though lately his night-time visits, hours of smoking and drinking and singing, had become less frequent. Zoë recalled the last time she'd seen him, out with Ingrid on his dory.

Ingrid. Never 'Mom' or 'Mommy'.

He took out his bone pipe and lit it with cupped hands and the smell reminded Zoë of cooking days at Red Bess's lighthouse, the fug of the fat woman's kitchen.

'Got time to see something?'

She nodded, and as they walked she could see the harbor curving below, shoddy and gray, full of chimney-heads billowing white peat smoke.

She wondered where Ingrid was.

Einar breathed hard climbing the hill, but here on the tops his stride was loose. He took her hand and led her up a steep path to a jut of crag and got onto his knees, beckoning. She crawled along to the lip, his hard hand on her back; she felt his strength. The white noise of the waterfall was intense and the river below was wide and had an orange-tinged clarity.

'There. See?'

A tree sprouted from the crag as if hewn from rock, clutching a colossal nest of twig and moss and grass and feather, whitewash splatter of guano down its trunk. Appearing from the nest, the creamy crown of a bird.

'Bald eagle,' Einar whispered. 'The nest is called an eyrie. There were three chicks at the start. Only one survives. Fittest.'

Zoë made a mournful noise, 'Ahw.'

'That's the daddy eagle. Mommy's out fishing capelin or hunting turtle or crab. They mate for life. Meet here every year. Same nest. The chick's about twelve weeks. Fly out any day now and I sure hopes to see it, more than anything.' Einar's scarlet face reflected some kind of miracle. He pulled Zoë back from the edge and they sat between some laurel bushes. 'I remember winters so cold,' he said. 'Birds falling frozen from their roosts. Geese imprisoned in ice.'

'Prisons of ice?'

He showed her his pistachio-colored teeth, and when he said *yeah* he inhaled the word, sucking it down like he was shocked.

'I found an iceberg once,' she said.

'You don't say.'

'Down on the bay. Bigger'n the cottage.'

'Huh. They usually bes running aground on Klibo. Usually hit the north island first. Don't touch down here as a rule.'

'Ingrid said I was probably the first human to touch it.'

He turned his head suddenly, hand to ear. 'You can hear the sea in the falls, like it's saying: I'm coming. Scrolls and harps of waves.'

He was right; there was a pulse and roll behind the thunge of water.

He plucked a piece of grass for her and she chewed it, salt-tasting. Then he picked a flower and slid it behind her ear, running his fingers through her hair. 'Silky as a calf's flank.'

She noticed a sea boil on his neck, bitty volcano ready to burst.

'Back to school next week. You must start going, you know.'

She pulled a face. 'Can we go swimming in the falls?'

Einar laughed. 'You're something.'

'Gonna be a fisherman when I grow up.'

'That right?'

'Yar.'

'You making fun of me?'

'*Yar.*'

'Asides, I can't go in the water,' Einar said. 'Can't swim.'

She pointed towards the horizon. 'But you *fish*.'

'If the sea wants you, she'll take you. Don't matter you swim or not.'

She pondered this for a moment. 'I made a wish,' she said. 'That would only come true once that berg on the beach had melted. And it *did* come true. Because when it melted there were a dead seal inside. Did you know my daddy?'

Einar squinted at his pipe for a moment. 'Never even knew my own daddy none. Drowned. Snowblindness. Over in Alaska.'

'Ingrid says my daddy were a *selkie*. Will you turn into a seal?'

He stared distantly, like he was tide-watching. He seemed as far away as the hillsome skyline, green eyes like tiny apples. 'Let's be making tracks,' he said.

Halfway down the causeway they came to a field of long grass swirling in a breeze Zoë could neither feel nor smell. In the glebe below women collected their washing from back gardens, bright colors billowing.

Einar touched her cheek. 'Head straight home now, afore the midges bite.'

She walked away with a smile on her face, taking the cut down past the cottage, and kept on walking. She saw the Dog Star making its appearance and a giggle bubbled in her throat, remembering something Einar said – he told her that the stars were shoals of fish. Constellations caught in me net. She headed down to the harbor to let her shoes get soaked in the landwash, antsy geese scratching and ruffling about her. Waiting, imagining the blue-black sky filling with Einar's haul.

INGRID WAS peering out the window wearing her stained dressing gown, wheat-colored hair coiled around her shoulders in thick, muscular whorls, breath fogging the pane. She spotted Zoë watching her and walked back into the darkness of the room.

Zoë stepped into the warmth of the house where the fire was banked, stoked, climbing high and spitting, drawing up the flue. Ingrid was stood looking at herself in the corridor mirror, pinching her cheeks until you could see the roses. Without turning to Zoë she asked, 'Am I beautiful? Do you think I'm still pretty?'

Zoë shrugged and walked past her and went into her room and got under the bed sheets and turned on the flashlight.

Ingrid shouted down the corridor: 'Don't be touching the fire, young lady. And don't answer the door to no one. You hear?'

In the circle of light Zoë stared at the image she had torn from a school library book: a man crouched on a snow-covered beach, his hand on the back of a fat seal.

She heard the front door slam shut and wrapped her arms around herself.

'Daddy.'

She opened the window and peered out, the town on Klibo softly illuminated on the distant headland. She eyed the black stretch of water separating the islands and wondered whether her father was hunting out there below the waves.

Later, a summer storm raged against the island and it felt like the cottage was at sea, an east wind goldering around the clapboard houses like a gang of vandals carrying blades. It tore through the harbor, smashing and riving, flinging doors hundreds of feet into the air. Zoë heard it wolf-whistling between the eaves and imagined Ingrid and Einar embracing.

A few days later Zoë wandered down to the Bay of Sotra to watch the beluga whales, surprised to find such a crowd huddled beneath the fading Aurora, bathed in the demi-light of its gossamer veils. She stood on her own where the rocks kissed the waves, staring out across the sea's sub-Arctic shell.

Whales arching white, finless backs.

Icebergs clunking on the horizon like bobbing refrigerators.

Eyes closed, she listened beyond the slow lop of waves and the sighs coming from the whales' blow-holes and heard the island's chronicle of pain. Snowmobiles, tabanasks, plunging through bay-ice, generations lost in dark wanderings amid frozen islands, beneath sishy drift, the lucky ones climbing out only to freeze to death. The dismal orchestra of their final yelps – she heard them all. *Sensitive*, they call it on the island.

Honeycombed flakes stroked her face, making her look down. The rocks between her boots were furred with petals of frost. She picked some, placing them in her mouth before setting off on her usual path to school through the tucka-more trees.

The classroom air was pungent with damp clothes and hair drying. Zoë stared through the fogged-up window, through the greasy smudge where her head usually lay, and the morning began to go by in its usual blur of daydream and staring-offs until the teacher said, 'Zoë, can you come outside for a minute?' He always pronounced her name like it was spelled Zowie.

All the children turned to her; it felt like they could read her mind.

The teacher opened the door into the cloakroom. 'Get on the go.'

He told her to take a seat on the bench and rubbed his hands down his gray trousers, ironed to a terse pleat. He sat so close to Zoë that she could read the patterns in his eyes, the blue blooms of irises.

He asked her about the mark on her face. She shrugged.

'I know some of the children are bigger'n you. Riving about at playtime. But all you got to do is come tell me. Tell me who's doing this and I'll be after making them stop.'

The sea had taken the teacher's wife and when he pushed the hair from Zoë's eyes she heard the ocean sounds within him, like pressing a shell to her ear.

'Everything OK at home?'

She jerked her head away.

'Listen on,' he said. 'I don't want you turning up to school all black and blue again or I'll be having words with your mom.'

She wanted to laugh out loud, watching her boots walk her back to her chair.

THE ALARMING quiet of the cottage was a whoosh in her ears. There was no indistinct blare resounding from the television and she hadn't heard Ingrid coming along the corridor yet. Zoë pictured Ingrid sat in her chair, staring at the wall, thinking her thoughts.

She got off the bed and went to the window. The rain had slacked but water still pitter-pattered onto the sill from the guttering. A gray dusk was settling over the harbor and a pale cusp of moon flashing through the cloud completed the view.

Some time later, the room was pitchy apart from a slither of light shrinking across the carpet: the door being closed.

She dug her thumb knuckles into her eye-pits and sat up in bed. She could smell bath oils and hear the suck of water going down the plughole. She listened in the darkness to Ingrid's heavy steps, the swish of the kitchen door opening, the slap of her feet on the tiled floor, the scrape of a chair being pulled from under the table. She imagined Ingrid's fingers passing through her thick, damp hair; her purple bunions protruding like baby beetroot from the insides of her milk-white feet; spider-hairy toes curled up against the cold; her wine-stained dressing gown wrapped around her body, still damp from the bath water. There was a chattering of kitchen sounds: steel against steel, pot against pan, bowl clunking against the wood of the table top.

Zoë dressed quickly and clambered out of her bedroom window.

There was a dead sheep by the track, the meat flensed off it, and she wondered what monster was up there, waiting for her in the hills of Asgard Fea. The Atlantic sky was a blue-black sheet, louring. The sheep started making their noises, stretching hind legs, dropping raisins from their holes. Einar called these lower slopes the Clearcut, because, he said, there used to be a forest here at one time, but all that was left now was rock and vegetation. She saw the dark shapes of the bird-hides where people came with their binoculars and guidebooks, and thought maybe she'd sleep in one of them tonight. But she kept on climbing, up between the gritstone tors, seeing bits of fleece stuck in the heather. She crossed the bridge over the stream and stopped to peer down, listen. Touching her bruises, she imagined her body swirling in the currents. She wondered how long she could stay up there, make Ingrid worry and regretful, knowing that soon, as always, she would return to the cottage. Mother and daughter, the strangest of dances.

But she wanted to be away from this place for good. From the claustrophobia of this tiny island. From all the things it held.

Not knowing that soon her wish would be granted.

Friday October 8, 1999

Zoë disappears

GUSTS ROSE vertically off the cliff-face, forcing Ingrid to cling onto the railings as she wended her way up to the lighthouse. Below, the sea was heaping.

Red Bess stood large in the doorway to Enchanted Lights, stout arms clasped around the hemisphere of her breasts. 'What a mess of a day,' she said, slamming the door behind them.

The shop was armpit-warm, with a heavy odor of heated soy and beeswax, birch bark tree sap and the after-scent of tallow; materials Ingrid used to make her candles. She smoothed the hair from her face.

Red Bess asked, 'Is Zoë sick?'

'Not that I know of.'

'The school's been on the phone. She's not been in all morning.'

Ingrid rubbed her eyes, her cheeks. 'She'll be ramping about on one of her little dilders, you know.'

'On a day like *this*?'

The two women looked towards the window where beaded raindrops twitched on the pane before being sucked out to sea.

'You should answer your goddamn telephone. Does she usually go off without a by-your-leave?'

Ingrid stared at Red Bess, blinking.

'She was seen down the harbor this morning, poor soul.'

'By who?'

'One of the kids. The principal thinks you better go looking.'

'Does she indeed?'

'She's only doing her job. Anyway, I'm shutting up for the day. No one in their right mind's coming up here in this.'

Ingrid looked back towards the window and then checked her watch: almost two. Another hour or so of daylight.

'You want to take the car?'

'No,' she said. 'Thanks.'

Red Bess patted Ingrid's arm. 'She'll be fine.'

She took the causeway down to the Sound, looking for the signature flash of Zoë's cherry-red macintosh. Nothing. Just a few seal heads watching her from Drifa Flow. Whitecaps scattered, foam streaked, crests turned spindrift. Force seven plus, Ingrid thought, and the blast of a trawler's horn startled her. She watched it for a moment, pitching and yawing over the waves, feeling sorry for the men onboard.

A day like this.

She walked along the pebbled beach, looking for a child's footprints in the sand, golden bladderweed popping beneath her feet. Turning the headland she could see the harbor, a shamble of pale weatherboard houses, eaves pointing seawards. Ingrid smiled, playing the scene in her mind: the words they'd share when she walked into the cottage and found Zoë spread out on the couch watching TV.

Ingrid searched the cottage high and low, checking closets, wardrobes, cupboards, piles of laundry, in and under the beds, anywhere Zoë could crawl and hide. The silence of the house never seemed so loud. Desperate.

She stood looking at the straw crosses above Zoë's headboard, to protect her from the trolls, the men of the Underworld. Her unmade bed of ruffled pink sheets. Moppy, her stuffed bunny, and the drawings on the walls. Had Ingrid ever spent this long in her daughter's room just looking?

She lifted Zoë's pillow to her nose. Syrupy. Unfamiliar.

She left the cottage and headed down the dark lanes towards the harbor. She stood for a while beside the wall where sea-wrack rose and fell like lungs. She spoke her daughter's name, just less than a shout, as if they were playing hide-and-seek, as if they ever played at all. She peered up into the spots of starlight and her voice swelled as she screamed across the harbor, 'Zoë?' Swallowed by the wind.

THE TWO Rangers stepped into the hallway and Ingrid saw the cottage through their eyes, the total mess of the place.

'Maybe you'd like to sit down.'

'I'm fine standing. Out with it.'

'We'd usually take longer assessing whether such a situation is critical or not, but due to Zoë's age . . .'

'Ten,' Ingrid shouted. 'She's only ten.'

'We've spoken to the principal. She's given us the name of the boy that saw her this morning. We've got Rangers interviewing him now.'

'Good. That's good.'

'Has she ever run away before?'

Ingrid swallowed, shrugged. 'No.'

'Did you have an argument?'

In the silence Ingrid remembered the last words she had with Zoë that morning; Zoë pulling a face, rubbing her stomach and saying, 'But I've a sore puggy.' Ingrid's bitter response.

'Could she be with friends?'

'Not that I know of. She's a bit of a loner.'

The fact struck her heart like a hammer.

'We're mobilizing a full search of the town as we speak. Houses, gardens. Is there anyone we can call?'

Ingrid turned towards the window. 'I'm going to kill her when I find her.'

'Zoë's father,' the female Ranger asked. 'Is there any chance . . . ?'

'No. There's no chance. Asides, he's no idea. He left the island before I knew I was carrying. Back to Norway. He's never been in touch.'

'What about a current partner?'

Ingrid sighed, shook her head.

'You got a recent photograph of Zoë we can use?'

The request felt brutal.

She walked over to the stone mantel where four photographs in cardboard frames leaned amid dust and clutter. She chose the one of Zoë in her uniform, taken at the beginning of the new school year a few weeks ago. She imagined Zoë waiting in line in the echoing hall as some tired photographer called child after child to sit on the chair before the speckled screen, to turn sideways and give that three-quarter profile. Say cheese. Zoë loathed having her picture taken.

Ingrid handed the photograph over, feeling she was misplacing part of herself.

'We'd like to search the house, if that's OK?'

'You're wasting your time.'

The Rangers nodded and moved into the other room.

Ingrid opened the front door. Rain blew in off Drifa Flow. She held her breath, trying to feel Zoë, and saw the school register in her mind, the space next to Zoë's name. The empty box that would come to haunt her.

*

Red Bess brought food with her. 'Take a bite before you leave,' she said.

'No,' Ingrid snapped.

'You've got to keep your strength up.'

'Stay here,' she said, 'so they know where to bring her.'

Outside, islanders wandered the lanes in small groups, throwing circles of flashlight behind hedges, into garages, anywhere a child could hide, calling Zoë's name. Every window of every house was illuminated.

Ingrid took the path up towards Brondhus Falls, Zoë's favorite place – waterfalls behind the town that charged in summer and froze like crystal staircases in winter. Inshore men were checking points along the island. Bay of Sotra. The Gloup. Unstad Beach. Asgard Fea, its summit covered in snow, a pale triangle up there. Check the cliffs, she'd told them. And we need to check the hills, take the horses. Better wait until first light, they said. Meaning it's too dangerous. Her little girl was out there, probably to spite her, and none of them knew that it was Ingrid's fault.

'Zoë?'

The wind swirled the field beside the track, creating sleepy, whispering sounds that made her stop to listen, as if they were some kind of augur. Nothing; just the choir of footsteps crunching and voices calling in that tone of inquiry. Why? How?

Be thankful for the full moon, Red Bess had said. But the sky was cloud-sodden and at times a halo formed around the disc, a broch. Ingrid knew how the islanders construed such signs, though being good churchgoing folk they never spoke the words anymore.

She wrestled the images in her head: Zoë huddled in a

cave on the mountain or lying smashed at the base of the Gloup. She's going to be freezing.

Ingrid closed her eyes, trying to feel for her. Nary an inkling.

A search has been launched for 10-year-old Zoë Nielsen who has been missing overnight since she failed to arrive at school on the island of Unnr. Island Ranger Aidan Marwick said they are investigating the possibility that Zoë may have run away from home. Ranger Marwick said Zoë, who attends Gulber Voe Junior School, has never been missing overnight before. She was last seen by a fellow pupil on his way to school at 08.40 hrs yesterday morning. Concerns were heightened after temperatures on the island fell to minus 13C overnight. Local people have been out all night looking for the girl. Zoë, who lives with her mother, Ingrid Nielsen, is described as being a 'shy' child . . .

THE OLD crofter's cottage overlooked the glebe that ran down to the Sound. In the distance the hills of Klibo rose from the sea to a height of over 800 meters. Behind the cottage, morning drizzle saturated 200 uniforms trudging through blanket bogs, climbing icy slopes, sitting aboard rescue dinghies and descending on ropes into the collapsed sea cave, the cavernous Gloup. The uniforms of army personnel and specialist search units from the mainland, joined by local Rangers and over 100 islanders and inshore men.

Suddenly everything was all about numbers.

Inside the cottage, Ingrid sat beside the fire, clothes steaming.

'Twenty-six hours,' she kept repeating. 'Just let her be found.'

Zoë is described as white, 4 feet 6 inches tall with shoulder-length blonde hair that was tied in pigtails. She is of slim build with green eyes. She was wearing a beige pleated front scooter with a blue gingham blouse and white knitted tights and a red macintosh coat with a fur-lined hood. She wore furry, chocolate-colored boots . . .

THE WOMAN stepped into the cottage, flanked by the two Rangers, Aidan and Anika. She introduced herself as Fay Larocque and shook Ingrid's hand. She had a French Canadian accent and was dressed like it was a Friday night with her coiffed hair and fur coat and a bit too much make-up.

Ingrid remained seated. She looked around the room and realized Red Bess had tidied up at some point.

'So you're from the mainland,' Ingrid said. 'Must think it's bad?'

Fay pulled up a chair and sat next to Ingrid. 'I'm a Family Liaison Officer.'

'And what's that when it's at home?'

Red Bess said, 'I'll get that tea poured,' and headed into the kitchen.

'I'm here to help maintain the integrity of the case.' Fay offered a compassionate smile. 'I need to gather as much information from you as I can, in the hope that this will contribute to the search. But mainly I'm here to identify your needs. To offer you support.'

Ingrid took a good look at the woman. 'What you mean—' she said, but didn't finish.

'So I need to put together a family tree, and we need to contact Zoë's father, to eliminate him from the inquiry.'

Ingrid, feeling the depth of time, opened her mouth, hesitated. 'Jon Tidemand. From Oslo. Second Officer. The vessel was called the *Geir*. I don't have an address. Thought it was just a summer fling, you know. I remember him saying he had an apartment overlooking Slottsparken, somewhere in the city. He said I'd like it there in the summer. Zoë hasn't been to Europe yet . . .'

Ingrid watched the woman writing it down and wondered where those words would end up, what kind of reaction they'd create, and how many lives they'd affect.

Red Bess appeared with mugs on a tray.

'The ship that left for Greenland yesterday,' Fay said. 'It was boarded and searched . . .'

'And?'

'I'm afraid Zoë wasn't on board.'

'What about the rest?'

Aidan and Anika whispered something to each other and Fay glared them back into their place. Red Bess handed Fay a mug of tea.

'Not every vessel is recorded,' Anika said. 'If we'd been alerted earlier . . .'

If I'd've been a better mother.

'And we've interviewed Einar,' Fay said.

'So the gossip's started?'

The three officers shared looks.

'We've got to pursue every line of inquiry,' Aidan added.

'You're barking up the wrong tree there.'

Aidan stepped forward. 'We're setting up an Incident

Room down at the harbor. We've been bombarded with possible sightings, both here and on Klibo.'

Ingrid rose and walked across the room and opened the door. Cameras flashed. People said her name. She stared down the glebe across the Sound towards the distant hills, then went back inside and got her Gore-Tex jacket, asking Red Bess to stay at the cottage.

'Where you heading?'

'Klibo. Stein. It hadn't occurred to me.'

'Take my cell phone,' Red Bess said. 'I'll call.'

Anika placed a hand on Ingrid's arm. 'We've got Rangers on Klibo already.'

'So what? You know me better'n that. I need to look for myself. You going to put me under house arrest?' Ingrid turned to Fay. 'Can you get rid of those people outside?'

'We need them,' she said. 'We'd like you to do an appeal later, on TV.'

'You're joking?'

'We think a personal appeal will help enormously.'

Ingrid looked towards the TV screen where Zoë's face had been appearing all morning, a stranger's voice describing her daughter in such detail.

Everything seemed so fake, so illusory.

'I need to look for myself,' Ingrid said. 'You can't keep me cooped up here. She's out there, I know it. I'll do it this afternoon, but she'll be back by then.'

'We'd prefer it if Fay went with you,' Anika said.

Ingrid looked at Fay's clothes and smiled.

Ingrid shuffled, poor-footing at the helm of Einar's drifter, stowing the final fender and staring out over Drifa Flow as the boat began lifting to the waves. A few gulls flew and hopped around the wooden deck in vain.

Einar came from the cockpit and passed Fay a yellow sou'wester, failing not to look at her legs. He told them there was a rough tidal-way surrounding the island. 'The journey'll take a bit longer than usual,' he said. 'And we're against the ebb.'

Ingrid wanted to talk to him alone, to find out what the Rangers had asked. The scarlet veins on his cheeks looked like a permanent blush; she usually found it endearing, but now it made him look like he had something to hide. She was minutely aware of how Fay watched them both.

She turned her back and stared overboard. The boat cut through the lumpy water, shock-like, trawl warps creaking. Dark, formless world below. Ingrid tried not to think about that afternoon's TV appeal, some kind of public acknowledgement that things were bad and getting worse.

She had clung to this very deck six months before while she and Zoë were out spotting the annual migration of humpback whales, the island disappearing behind them as the boat yawed and a wind full of moisture shunted through the rigging. Ingrid pointing, 'Look!' A fin as large as the side of a house, water spraying from a blow-hole. Zoë clapping, squealing, Einar holding her hand, pointing out the animal's fluke-holes as the horizon disappeared completely.

Ingrid would encourage Zoë to explore the island on her own. 'You're a girl,' she'd say. 'You got to do what *you* want in this world. Be free.' Like Zoë needed any encouragement. She preferred being on her own and in many ways she was the adult of the house. Ingrid would suggest things they could do together, taking her on drawing trips deep into the hills, nature walks along the beach. Zoë would never show Ingrid what she had drawn. The place that was Zoë's head, it seemed, was so much more interesting than the world it had to travel through. As a result Zoë gained a fierce independence, but one that was so totally unsympathetic. Ingrid found this hard to fathom.

It was at this moment that she felt the breach in her defenses, worn-out tears lost in the moisture sluicing through the rigging, sobs obscured by the friction of the boat slapping — for it was, she imagined, the boat's transom grating over Zoë's body.

Her disloyal fears stunned her.

Then the flag luffing was her dead mother pinning the washing out on a blustery day. Ingrid wondered what her mother would do, how she would act in this situation. Whatever her mother's choices, they would be better than hers.

Fay began to retch against the gunwale.

Within half an hour they were cruising along the coastline of Stein, a tiny island populated by a feral herd of beef cattle, ruined cottages and tillage land, a few wind-stunted trees. The enormous wooly longhorns watched them from the shore like Viking warriors spoiling for a fight.

Land smells wafted in, a blend of juniper and cow shit.

Ingrid felt no kinship to the waves. She thought about all the fishermen she knew that had been stolen by the sea. Her father, a man she couldn't remember, taken with sixteen crew off the coast of Cape Farewell. You live on an island for so long and you come to believe the sea hates all human life.

And she wished, not for the first time, that her mother were still alive.

We are continuing to appeal for anybody who saw anything suspicious yesterday to get in touch. We are also asking islanders to think about anyone they know who appears to have been behaving out of the ordinary. Anyone with information should contact the Rangers' office on . . .

SHE WOULD remember a room full of people and cameras flashing; sudden, grave silences; the press being so present there wasn't room for anything else; the way her fingers shook against her cheeks; hearing a voice and listening to a voice and being surprised that it was her voice; Fay like a shadow beside her. People would say that Ingrid looked harsh and defensive that day. People would say that she looked guilty.

Will Zoë see this? Will she hear how sorry I am?

And Ingrid would wonder whether she did the TV appearance at all that day because she wanted to be humiliated, strangers' eyes spotlighting her neglectfulness.

She woke up in Zoë's bed, holding Zoë's hairbrush. She sniffed her daughter's scalpy, cordite smell, listening to Red Bess and Fay talking in the other room. She climbed out of bed and went to the window. In the darkness she could make out a liner's funnels and they told her that life was continuing out there, though it felt like her life had stopped.

She turned and looked at the room, remembering the first time she felt Zoë move inside her, how life's focus shifted inwards. The day she brought Zoë home from the hospital and watched her, two days old, taking the blanket off and blowing her, Zoë's head moving against her neck. Realizing the presence holding her hand was that of her mother. Three female echoes in the room. Karita, her mother suggested, it means loving and benevolent. But Ingrid didn't want an island name, full of portent. She wanted a name that was strong, simple, exotic.

Ingrid cricked her neck to see the moon outside. It reminded her of a scene from a movie and she realized it was the movie of her life.

A movie she didn't want to watch anymore.

ZOË KNEW that she was below ground and no one would hear her but still she screamed for help, her knuckles a scabby pulp from punching the walls. The machine breathed into the room, its constant whine and rattle niggling her. This was her first week in captivity, an animal in a cage waiting to be fed and watered, for the man to reappear. Or were there more than one?

She found the sink and twisted the faucet but no water came and so she drank from the toilet bowl.

Sudden light. The tiny room was bare. Nothing on the walls, no windows.

Darkness.

The rush of air on her skin. Hands and knees and legs around her.

'Ingrid!'

The smell of this man driving pain into her.

'IT DOESN'T make me feel any better, looking at these. How come each day I feel worse and all you or anyone else says is "don't give up hope, it'll get better." I'm dead inside. You get to the bottom and you think this is the lowest I can possibly go but then another hole opens up and you fall. It doesn't stop. I'm just a ghost going from room to room, listening for her. You know, I can't even remember who I was before I gave birth to her. I was so young. I don't know how I can go on without her.'

'But you have to,' Red Bess said. 'For Zoë's sake.'

The hours passed far too quickly, too vividly.

'Someone's taken her and I'll never see her again. I know it. I'm a failure. I just want it all to end.'

This was how Ingrid was talking, lying curled up in a ball on Zoë's bed. She'd just had that dream again, of a ship sailing over the island, cutting deep grooves into the hillsides; she knew what it meant and she'd been crying so hard it felt like she'd damaged her internal organs. Red Bess stayed with her, listening to her orderless babble and refusing her sheet-twisting demands for more sleeping pills and Newfy screech. Sobriety was no way to confront this, a kind of death that forbids grieving. Scattered on and around the bed were Zoë's drawings.

'I was never here. Such terrible thoughts I'm having.'

The curtains were muted to the outside world and Red Bess kept the fire going in the front room. Einar brought fresh peat every evening, knocking on the back door three times to signal his presence. Ingrid refused to see him. Just the same, Red Bess would tell him. He'd nod and walk away, head hangdog.

'But Zoë didn't need friends, she had her imagination.'

Ingrid would never forget that moment Fay Larocque told her it had turned from a missing person's inquiry to a murder investigation. It had become a search where no one wanted to find what they were looking for. Every house, every inch of moor, beach, cliff, even the nearest towns on the mainland were searched and re-searched, but still Ingrid felt they weren't doing enough.

'I can see her face. Can hear her moving about the house, humming. Can hear her moving through me.'

The newshounds were conspicuous in their absences, and the concerned voices of islanders at the door were lost to her. They were holding services at the church, special prayers. Ingrid declined the invitation.

This used to be an island where no one locked their doors, where children could walk to school alone. But no more. Now they walked in convoys, regularly updating their parents on their whereabouts on cell phones. It was Ingrid's fault.

The hunt continues for Zoë Nielsen who has been missing now for 17 days . . .

That sickening loop in her head.

'YOUR MOTHER'S dead. I'm in charge now. You obey *me*.'

Blood pooling in her cheeks. 'You're lying.' She spat it at him.

Head a sharp twist, a crack in her neck. She could no longer feel the pain.

'Ingrid's alive.'

'You call me "Sir"!'

Zoë knew, like every child knows, what this adult wanted and needed her to be. She also knew, instinctively, that disappointing him in this would be the worst thing she could do. But he'd have to fight her for it. In his voice she heard his weakness, and his weakness was that he wanted her.

It was her only way out. Trick him. She smiled her bloodied teeth at him.

'Yessir.'

He showed her the knife and then ran its serrated length gently across her neck. He went behind her, cut the ropes and released her from the chair. Then he punched her between the shoulder blades and she fell to her knees. He slipped a leash over her head and yanked the choker, blood dripping thickly from her mouth.

She closed her eyes. Don't give in. Opened them.

A bowl of dog food. A bowl of water.

'Eat, bitch.'

And she prayed that if she didn't see sunlight again she would turn the same shade of gray as the concrete walls and be rendered invisible and she would be able to slip past him through the door and to her escape.

Her world being rewritten.

Zoë Nielsen fading into the silence, the loneliness, the violence of the bunker.

She said, 'Don't leave me here.'

A THOUGHT appeared to settle upon Ingrid's face. She dashed across the room and fell to her knees in front of a chest of drawers and started pulling things out: old chandler's tools, greasy brown boxes. Then she froze.

Red Bess asked, 'What is it?'

Ingrid got to her feet and carried something over, never taking her eyes off the object in her hands. It was a small wooden jewelry box with a silver inlay pattern of a whale. Inside the box was a white handkerchief. Inside the handkerchief were small baby teeth.

Ingrid laughed through her tears.

'I told Zoë the elves had taken them.'

ZOË REGISTERED her movement, the pressure on her feet, butt, spine, hands on the concrete floor. Her senses were so heightened it was painful and the temperature in the room seemed to fluctuate but there was no visible heating except the recessed light above. She realized it was her body heat, the room much hotter after she slept. Hot air passed over her nostrils, itching. She thought she heard him over the speakers he had just fitted, along with the camera in the top corner of the room. She hummed another rhyme, touching the lump in her hairline where he'd knocked her out. She had begun to pray in these final moments, though she knew God couldn't hear her below. Did the world think she was dead? Had Ingrid packed her things away in boxes? She stood in the darkness and screamed towards the direction of the lens, calling him all the names she knew before collapsing onto the floor. I will die this day. Her breath: a dry, hard rasp,

INGRID WOKE to an empty house and the thud of knocking. She stood in the hallway for a moment looking at the snow-drift of letters building against the front door. She thought it must be Einar but there was an old woman stood there wearing a knitted caul and a man's ratty greatcoat. An easterly brought the smell of fish from the harbor.

'May I come in?'

'What you want?'

The old woman shuffled past her, stiff-jointed into the front room where she opened her coat and warmed her belly in front of the fire. 'I'm cursed with the Sight,' she said, her voice scratching like an old record. 'I've been getting visions recently. Of Zoë.' Strands of hair, part brown, part incandescent silver, sprang from the pins holding her caul in place.

'This some kind of sick joke?'

'And I know you got the curse too.'

'Get out.'

'I can teach you how to open your mind again.'

'I don't *want* to open my mind again.'

'I've been so switched on for the past three weeks it's painful.'

Ingrid stepped towards the door. 'Come on. Out.'

'Give me your hands.'

'Do you want me to call the Rangers' office?'

'They've already approached me for help.'

Ingrid paused. 'You're a liar.'

The old woman raised her brows.

'What,' Ingrid asked, 'so this is some kind of *ganfer*? Island omen?'

'*Ganfer* indeed. I've seen her. And many *foregings*. I've heard the ticking of the woodworm. The dead-shak of the quail. Death can still be avoided. Give me your hands.'

Ingrid laughed bitterly. 'Where you from?'

'Your skin.'

'My skin?'

'Let me touch you.'

'You're a witch.'

Rheumy eyes blinking. 'I come from Stein.'

'No one lives there.'

'I knew your mother well.'

A few seconds lingered in the air that stretched Ingrid's lungs. She told herself to breathe, exhaling raggedly. She laid her hands on the woman's palms.

'Trapped,' the old woman said. 'Immersed in darkness. Silence.'

'Where?'

'She's bound. Cold. Alone. You know it's your fault.'

Ingrid said weakly, 'How dare you.'

'Get your coat.'

Zoë Nielsen sighting prompts interest. Claims that a girl calling herself 'Zoë' was seen in the USA recently. An Ohio gas station attendant, Frank McDormand, 53, said the girl said 'he took me from my mommy'. Zoë vanished aged 10 in October this year while on her way to school. The attendant claims he spoke to the girl who resembled Zoë and who was accompanied by a man who appeared 'uncomfortable' . . .

WALKING DULL hills and slippery cliff-edges before dawn, away from meddlesome eyes, feet slithering over seaweedy shale and sphagnum rock, reading the sea's moods as fluky winds pushed and slapped her, making their way down from Greenland. Ingrid would walk right to the far edges of the island, watching the brightening eastward skies, out to the sea-stack they called Unnr Castle, willing it to fall, to crumble into the sea, wanting to topple it with her bare hands. Then she'd walk back to the lighthouse, its optic giving out six flashes every thirty seconds. Island heartbeat.

Does she know how much I love her? I hope so.

One morning there was a sudden storm and she sought shelter in a derelict barn with a corrugated roof. Death seemed to be drifting across the island right then, filling every pore with its rotten winds.

Was it my fault she never asked for anything?

Time creased and folded, making a paper airplane that she held like a pen and jettisoned into the salt-sprayed air, gulls hovering on an updraft beside her. It made sense to her, teetering here on the cliff-edge, wishing the wind would lift her into the air and throw her to rocks below.

To be with you.

Last week she followed the old witch down to the Bay of Sotra in something like a trance. They stood between the tidemarks, between good and evil. Above them, Cassiopeia circled Polaris upside-down. But the stars were just peepholes in the sky. The witch drew a circle around Ingrid in the sand and walked towards the shoreline and threw coins into the waves. Ingrid remembered hearing noises in the darkness between the witch's chants and a sudden flash made her check the horizon. Lightning, she thought, bringing her back into the present. Fuck this. She stepped from the circle and headed home.

They published Ingrid's photograph the next day, her face looking demented beside the word WITCHCRAFT. Community tensions were running high and she wondered had the old woman been a set-up. There was speculation in the press that charges would be brought against Ingrid. But gradually the snap and drool of the press pack dwindled and the calls and visits came in streaks and the silences between them communicated one message: fear had won.

Zoë was dead.

She would never be a young woman.

Have a first date.

Fall in love.

Choose a career.

Grow into her beauty.

Become a mother.

It was unlikely that Zoë had drowned, Ingrid was told. The waters around the island were too cold for decomposition, for the stomach to ferment. Zoë yeasting up. A body would simply float and be washed ashore. A child can disappear at a mile a minute, they added, and it was always a man that had taken her, he had stolen her and done unspeakable acts and killed and buried her where no one would find her. The ebb and flow of rumored sightings; Zoë was seen being bundled into a blue car, a red car, a BMW, a Ford pulling a white trailer; she was spotted on the decks of boats from Greenland all the way down to Cape Fear. There was talk of satanic abuse, of dirty old men in raincoats. Worry became scandal, became blame, became hatred, became that *thing* that we don't talk about anymore.

Every time Ingrid saw a child Zoë's age it would avert its gaze or run away, a parent pulling it near.

'There's that Ingrid Nielsen. She still thinks her daughter's alive.'

Even Red Bess had become distant; she said she was busy at Enchanted Lights, tourism was up and Ingrid's candles were selling well. Ingrid tried not to dwell on the reason why. And she refused to see Fay Larocque anymore.

She walked one more length of Unstad Beach as a skither of snow began to fall, but she didn't even notice; her imagination had become a torment: Zoë's body in her mind, bobbing in slow sea-time, her dusty-blonde locks, waveform, suspended. Zoë snagged below the waves on a sunken grappling hook.

I will never see you get married.

Ingrid walked broken, up the glebe towards the cottage, telling herself not to look over at the graveyard where her mother lay. Every time she walked up the lane, she imagined she would find Zoë inside the house, lying on the settee, watching TV, laughing. Waiting for a miracle.

But today she found a man standing at her door.

Haloed within his parka hood: a semblance of Zoë's face.

She had always pictured him standing at the helm, stars dazzling amid corals of cloudbank, listening to porpoise blowing and rolling beside the boat. And he would be thinking about her, about their nights together during the summer of 1988.

He'd come back to her across that watery desert. Time had changed him little. That periwinkle glitter to his eyes, showing so great against the sea-weathered skin and gingery stubble, the blond hair that couldn't be controlled.

Zoë was in those eyes.

Ingrid felt the quiver and dimple of her chin. To smile she had to unscrew her features, a real conscious effort, and with it the knowledge of how awful she must look. She finger-combed her hair and then covered her face.

He touched the skin on the back of her hands; she flinched.

'Ingrid.'

And the one thing that bound them both, the shadow of a ten-year-old girl, swooped between them for a moment as Ingrid moved into him.

DREAMS OF cliff-faces, of waves glutting against huge sea rocks, of caves that sucked and bellowed. Zoë heard a clipped, curt style of speech littered with dialect and saw stone jars along a dusty hearth, wind soughing among the eaves and down the chimneybreast, the intimate smell of peat blowing around the room.

She dreamed that she was looking through her old bedroom window, down the glebe across the Sound towards the hills of Klibo, beneath a bright moon that was tilting the sea. She heard Ingrid's and Einar's voices in the other room followed by the sound of seabirds outside, stabbing and slicing the air with their cries. Einar's laughter. That gentle fisherman she loved being around. But then she saw Ingrid standing waist-deep in a sea so black and so still it appeared matt, seaweed falling from her mouth, skin coated in limpet shells. Lichen beard. She looked like a mythical sea-troll. Ingrid pointed out to sea and gasped, Zoë looked but there was nothing out there. Then Ingrid turned to Zoë with eyes pitted, skull empty.

Zoë bolted awake with a gasp, blinking into the perfect darkness.

'Hello? You there? Sir? Hello? *Hello?*'

JON SHIFTED his weight around Zoë's bedroom like a man unsure of solid ground. Ingrid listened to him breathing, swallowing. Eleven summers before, they had made Zoë in this very room. Ingrid was nineteen, Jon twenty-four. He stopped beside Zoë's bed and stroked the ear of her stuffed bunny. Ingrid noticed a fresh-looking tattoo on the back of his hand.

'Moppy,' Ingrid said. 'She can't sleep without her Moppy.'

He threw her a glance.

She had forgotten about his mercurial eyes, how sometimes they appeared to hold all the water he had ever seen, shining a pale, Pacific blue; at other times, his head against the pillow, they appeared a matt, Arctic gray. It was chameleon-like, untrustworthy, but fascinating.

He was no longer boyish, but still she coveted his long white eyelashes and straight, wheat-colored hair. She wondered how come some men get better with age, like laughter lines and gravity had lent his face more intelligence, softened him somehow. The lines said here is a man who understands life better than you, and laughter, and, most probably, love.

'I've seen her picture on TV,' Jon said. 'But I'd like to see more.' His flawless English with that lilting, sing-song cadence.

Ingrid walked into her bedroom and took the photo album from her dresser top and sat on her bed, listening to him move through the hallway.

She patted the space beside her; clearing his throat, he came and filled it.

She passed him the album, staring at the tattoo of a full-rigged ship that almost covered the back of his hand. She knew what it signified: he'd sailed Cape Horn, the tip of southern Chile. The sailors' graveyard.

'She rarely cries,' Ingrid said. 'Even as a baby she'd just whimper for a bit and then – well, nothing. She's not aware of it, but she hums to herself all the time. Not loud, just background noise. For comfort, I guess.'

'But what's she like?'

Ingrid mellowed in his gaze. 'In what way?'

'As a person?'

She stared out the window into the Atlantic sky, wanting Jon to experience the scale of Zoë's absence contracting in the room around them, for Jon to feel its appalling ache, its gravity.

'When was this taken? She looks so happy.'

The six-year-old girl in the photograph, a chubby girl wearing a tight orange sweater and denim skirt and multi-colored, stripy tights, was pulling a face, coquettish almost. But Ingrid remembered a girl who looked different to the girl in the photograph. She remembered a girl who seemed to be forever frowning. A girl who smelled of sour milk and sphagnum moss. A girl who sat beside her window at dusk, drawing the gloaming world outside, using white chalk on black paper, like she had some preternatural gift for capturing darkness. An innate talent Ingrid envied.

Ingrid peeled back the film, removed the photograph and pressed it into Jon's hand. 'Take it. It's yours.'

Again, Zoë smiled out of his face.

She asked, 'How long can you stay?'

As old island custom decreed, her mother used to disappear whenever Jon stayed. 'I won't have him climbing through windows,' she said, 'or sit listening to you two going at each other all night.' One evening Jon found nettles beneath the bed sheets. 'My mother,' was Ingrid's explanation.

His final week, that summer eleven years before, they lay in bed listening to sounds coming in through the open window: the low putter of engines in the harbor; twitters of song sparrows on the neighboring moor; the distant hish of waves dying against the beach. She found herself ensnared in moments when those three words were almost out of her mouth. He would put a finger to her lips and say, 'I like you too. A lot.'

Then on the final night she was sure he mouthed it.

'What?' she asked.

He repeated it out loud, enunciating each syllable: 'Colorful.'

It looked so much like I love you.

The following morning she stood on the front doorstep of the cottage, watching him get smaller as he headed down the glebe. He never looked back. She imagined him walking along the quay, up the gangway, perhaps turning for one final look at the harbor. She read his home address once and threw it onto the fire, regretting it instantly. She searched her room to see if he had forgotten anything, a shirt or T-shirt that she could wear in bed, to smell him on her, around her. Just his absence. 'Why pretend it's something it's not,' her mother said. 'Menfolk are bad enough, but seamen, sailors, fishermen — they're a different breed entirely.'

Three months later, after ample denial, she confirmed Jon had indeed stayed. Lodged himself inside her. Knitting cells full of color.

Quebec Police have launched a huge search for the missing youngster Zoë Nielsen following a reported sighting by a French couple . . .

TWO DAYS after Jon's surprise arrival Ingrid was walking
through the sludgy streets alongside him but the journey
out felt a little fake to her and she was determined no silence
would fall between them, so she was talking her face off,
because there were eleven years of catching up to do, and
it was also a Friday, the day of the week that Zoë disappeared. But this Friday was the worst because Zoë had been
missing exactly one month: November 8 1999.

They were being watched.

Ingrid recognized what the woman staring out of the
butcher's window was thinking; and the elderly fisherman
who had been friends with her father; and the postman
doing his rounds on his son's BMX – she was privy to
their thoughts: Who's that man? Do you think . . . ?
Dragging her shame through the streets, fearful that by
the time she got home there would be nothing left of
her.

They continued to walk. Last night's snowfall was melting
in the crisp November sunlight, igniting a thousand icicles
dripping onto salty streets. The snow had composed rooflines
that were soft, diffuse. It hemmed in the streets, making

them feel narrower. All around was the rumble of big-assed trucks clearing snow.

She stole a glance at him and wondered if his body looked the same, remembering the hot abrasiveness of his kiss, the saltiness of his skin, the heavy, carved feeling of his muscles.

'When Zoë does well at school, or does a great drawing, or just does anything that she's really proud of and makes her feel good about herself, then I feel I'm a good mother, that I'm a *good enough* mother. But when things go wrong . . .'

They were approaching the harbor, stacks of wooden lobster traps filling the sidewalk.

'When you lose someone, a mirror is held up to you. Look, it says. Look at who you weren't.'

Ingrid stopped, pointed. *Have you seen this girl?* A poster of Zoë was pinned to the noticeboard on the wall and it saddened Ingrid because the girl in the photograph was already beginning to fade. 'There's no trace of her. No footprints. No signs of struggle. Just that last sighting of her walking here alone. And the young boy that saw her, he can't remember the expression on Zoë's face. And I want to know that more than anything because I'd shouted at her that morning and I know it's selfish but I want to know she wasn't crying. That she didn't walk into the sea with her pockets full of stones.'

'I think the Rangers could be doing more.'

Ingrid threw him a look, and though she didn't know it yet, that look contained their future. He'd even asked if he could see the spurious ransom notes and letters from people that claimed to have seen Zoë, in Labrador, in British Columbia, as far away as North Africa.

Today's horoscope said 'outside influences tend to throw you off track'.

The cold made Jon's eyes blaze.

'They said that if she got to the mainland,' her voice was almost lost, 'she could be anywhere. A mile a minute, they said. A child can disappear at *a mile a minute,* Jon.'

He made no reaction.

'I want to search the whole world but where do you start? I'm scared that if I leave Gulber that I won't be here for her when she returns. And I feel close to her here, surrounded by her things. It gives me hope, Jon. *Hope.*'

'Work. They said I could take as much time as I need.'

She fought the smile.

'For Christmas, I mean.'

She nodded, blinked. Almost three months by then.

But he had yet to ask that question.

He served the meal and opened a bottle of wine, such a simple act filling her with remorse: how dare you eat a nice meal and drink wine when your daughter is missing? He sat opposite her and smiled a smile as wiry as his limbs and fell to his food. Ice-filled rain pearled the windows so heavy and thick it made a slopping noise, skeins of the stuff sticking to the glass — a sleepy sound.

'Bitter rain tonight,' he said.

She nodded. It would be getting dark soon and again there would be this terrible hush lining the cottage. Don't leave. The candles threw sinister flickers around the room. His eyes were beady, obsidian. It was like he'd never been away.

'There are things I've seen,' he said. 'Things I ain't got words for.'

Head canted to one side, she threw him a smile that wasn't a smile. 'You should tell Zoë this. You should write your experiences down for her. For when she returns.' Because I know you won't be here.

He examined his hands. The room seemed to tilt. 'Sorry,' she said.

'We hunted seals,' he said. 'Front herd. The herd splits in two.'

'I know.'

'Course.'

'My father was a swiler. I told you that.'

The man Ingrid's mother referred to as He-Who-Was-Taken, like speaking his name would do him wrong in death. Whenever Ingrid thought about this man that she couldn't remember, she pictured him wearing an old, long Hudson's Bay coat, and pretended she could recall its thick woolen weave, the smell of tobacco and beer and ice clinging to it. But the one fact about her father that really brought him to life was that he had a piece of metal lodged in his skull from a motorbike accident that made him sensitive to barometric changes. He could feel storms coming before anyone could spy them through a lens. It was one of these storms that took him. Ingrid was three years old when he died at sea, and her mother made her lay a hand upon his head, or as she put it: 'upon his dust'. Beside Ingrid's bed, hanging from a hook on the wall, she kept her father's old compass, a wrist compass worn like a watch, given to him by a Russian naval captain.

'That's before Greenpeace stuck their oar in,' Ingrid said.

'And people got color TV.'

'Eh?'

'Color. The color of so much blood in people's living rooms.'

Ingrid glared at him, sighed.

'Whitecoats scattered across the ice,' he said. 'The blood. And the deck piled with pelts. Men sleeping among them. I'll never forget that smell. Sick-smelling.'

The whitecoats' blood, the color of Zoë's red macintosh.

'I keep having this dream,' she said, 'that I'm vomiting bones. One by one, day after day, I wake to find an extra bone on the floor. Her skeleton . . .'

The bob of his Adam's apple, a stony yo-yo in his throat.

'My brain won't allow me to imagine being without her.'

He nodded his large head.

'The things that I've started to remember, about Zoë as a baby. Funny little details, like her hiccuping breast milk down my neck. The smell of it. The intimacy.'

He blinked rapidly.

'And the way she'd always fill her diaper just as I was about to leave the house. And the way she'd kick me when I cleaned her. She even gave me a black eye once. And the way she always burped and smiled once she'd finished feeding. And if I dozed off while holding her, she'd try to prize my eyelids open with her sharp, tiny fingernails, and, as soon as she began to talk, she would point at random men in the street and shout . . .'

After a moment he said, 'Shout what?'

She could no longer make out the color of his eyes.

'She would shout . . . "Daddy".'

The Braille of his tattooed skin, feeling how he had aged, the soft spread of midsection between the sharp ridges of his hipbones. He kissed her forehead, her cheek. She offered him her mouth. They kissed hard, twisting. The solace of touch from a past lover, the illicit thrill, a contact that closed the space between them, the size of a ten-year-old girl. He placed his mouth against her nipple and she experienced his tongue in her brain, tickling awake the memories of Zoë suckling, the sensation and memory fused with lust. He spat onto his hand; she lifted her pelvis. He entered the dark space she had become.

Afterwards, she left the cottage and stood in the lane outside, surrounded by the heavy moisture of a winter snow-storm. Shivering, she remembered how she used to be so scared of the snow as a girl, how it used to fall so heavily, crystal arms linking, creating a woven blanket. The entire planet, she'd imagine, had become a giant snowball, and everything, the whole world, would be forgotten.

She couldn't see the harbor or the mountains of Klibo or any star, but out there, below the waves, she knew Zoë lay, waiting.

She headed back inside, thinking she didn't know this man at all.

Swedish holidaymakers claim to have seen a girl resembling missing Zoë Nielsen in the Moroccan city of Marrakesh. The police have been unable to locate the girl seen by the Swedish tourists . . .

THE FEAR never subsided. Often mistaking the trickle of tears in her ears for insects Zoë would bat them away and then lick her fingers, half-comforted by the taste of herself. These never-ending days below. Her memories were being eaten away by the silence and so she hummed to herself to remind her whose skin she was in. Food nightmares began to haunt her. In these nightmares the man would be serving her beefsteak and she would fall to it ravenously only to find he had sewn her mouth closed and she would bang the hot, pink flesh against her stitched, bleeding lips.

The man removed weeks, months. Her life parenthesized by these nameless, endless nights. Though there were nights she would lie on her back on the concrete floor and blink into the darkness and see stars, entire constellations, and the Aurora billowing below them like smoke, and lunar haloes like irises – Ingrid keeping a watchful eye on her. But mostly her own breathing and humming was all she heard for days.

INGRID WOKE herself up mewling. That dream again, of the empty tick box next to the name: Nielsen, Zoë. But the tick box was coffin-shaped, Zoë-shaped, slowly filling with soil, each day a handful more. Ingrid's dreams filling with earth.

It was Christmas morning, 1999. Seventy-eight days.

They sat on the living room floor together last night, wrapping Christmas presents for their missing daughter.

She had forgotten to close the curtains and the fragile demi-light told her it must be around 10 a.m. She could only remember fragments of last night.

The oil in the heater began to tick . . . tick . . . tick . . .

She had imagined Jon's death in detail many times. He would be fishing bowhead whales with natives when a rogue wave would catch him on the beam and drag him overboard. Ingrid imagined herself leaning over the gunwale, the creak of the ship filling the silence between her shouts. 'Jon? Jon!'

The sheen of sweat across his back glittered. Greasy exudate.

When he touched her, she felt like he was measuring, weighing. He squeezed and probed and ate upon her. She remembered making love to him that first time and the smell of fish. But Jon didn't make love, he consumed.

Zoë's shiny presents beneath the tree. They listened to the compilation tape she had made Zoë, and at one point, listening to Joni Mitchell's 'Woodstock', he began to weep. Ingrid couldn't bring herself to touch him.

There was something so elaborate about the shape of his skull, and the unhealthy way his eyes were too close-set. Scandinavian inbreeding; a part of his inheritance Zoë escaped. Ingrid scanned his sleeping body, the blue-black map of his sailings, the fresher tattoos in deep reds and periwinkle blues: the pig on one foot and a rooster on the other; the anchor on his shoulder blade and the shellback turtle on his buttock; the rope around his wrists and the sparrow beneath his left ear. She read them like portents, because below them were his organs. Blood. Tissue. Ligaments. Brain. Bones. Marrow. DNA. They were in part Zoë's, but he was here, beside, inside, breathing, beating, alive. She hated him for it.

Anyone walking on the moor could have seen them through the movie screen of her window last night, but no one ever walked the moor behind the house, only Einar. Jon said he'd heard two inshore men gossiping down by the harbor, talking about her and Einar. 'But that's none of my business,' was his answer to her glare.

In case Zoë came home last night. Christmas Eve. Something to open.

His snore, like a rope luffing against a mast. She wanted to slap him awake. Finally he stirred, nuzzling into her, placing his face against her stomach. Life in the room paused. He opened his mouth and she dared him to say it. Merry Christmas. In the silence a liner blew its horn and she heard the word: Mom. Then she felt a hand on her breast.

She pushed him away and climbed out of bed, taking her father's wrist compass from the wall, and headed into the bathroom. Through the westerly window she could see the mountains of Klibo, so lucid in their snowiness. She fastened the compass to her wrist and tried to imagine the white-coats scattered across the ice, but instead she saw Zoë's corpse rotting in slow ice-time amid the crack and boing of transferring ice sheets.

Ingrid pressed her face against the mirror because she knew it was the coldest object in the room. Colorful, she mouthed to her reflection.

Three knocks on the bathroom door. 'Ingrid?'

They dressed and left the cottage in silence, the wind making it almost impossible to close the front door. Here they met Red Bess huffing up the lane.

'Have you heard?' she asked.

Ingrid walked in determined confusion towards the Rangers' office, trying to listen.

'But it was the butcher's son saw him being led away. Handcuffed.'

She heard Christmas carols being played. Saw portholes rubbed in steamed-up windows, faces peering out.

She knew what Jon was thinking. He was thinking this is it, this is our man. That Ingrid had not been telling the truth. That she had lied to him about her relationship with Einar Reed. She knew that everyone in this dumb town would think he did it. But she knew he didn't do it. She climbed the steps to the jailhouse telling herself: Einar did not do this.

Rangers on the island of Unnr have detained a Gulber Voe man accused of abducting 10-year-old Zoë Nielsen. In a news release last night, the Rangers' office confirmed Einar Reed is accused of taking Zoë from near her home in Gulber Voe on October 18. The 43-year-old is lodged in the Gulber Voe Jailhouse . . .

'I'LL MAKE a proper woman out of you.'

It was as if he knew everything about her, like he could read her mind, like he knew she was beginning to forget the details of Ingrid's face and could no longer close her eyes and summon the length or color of Ingrid's hair. She tried refusing to speak, refusing to get out of bed. He pinched her. No response. He punched her, slapped her. Not even a murmur. So with his clasp knife he sliced a groove out of the sole of her foot and then hit the wound with a stick. Brutal bastinado. She quickly found she had a voice.

He started to bring things down to her, sheets, a pillow, clothes, but the clothes must have been dimestore-bought because they were horrible.

He showed her how to clean herself in the sink and then stood watching her undress. She would have to dry everything with a towel, the sink and faucets and any splashes on the floor. He would even make her dry the soap afterwards and position it in such a way and God help her if she got it wrong. The threat of harm was always right there, above her, on her, in her. He brought her a book, an encyclopedia, and when the light was on she read it over and over. He even brought a teddy bear and then one day a couple of real live brown-black puppies. The joy she felt was stupefying. She learned later they were coydogs, a mix of coyote and mongrel, half-tame, half-beast. He left them with her for over an hour before taking them away, laughing.

INGRID WAS so used to coming down here alone, away from prying eyes, searching along the beach for Zoë's body. But it had been over a month since she'd done her laps of the island. Instinctively she checked the coastline for a spot of red and wished that it were now, with Jon beside her, that their daughter's body was washed ashore.

New Year. A new millennium. Ingrid had stopped counting the days.

It snowed solidly that week but still the sky looked heavier than the earth. In places the exposed, wind-smoothed sand appeared glass-like. Further out, gannets plunged and pregnant she-seals twisted through lumpy pack ice. And about a mile out, a solitary berg plied the waves, the size of a two storey house, unmoored from its Arctic shelf.

Ingrid and Jon's shared gaze across this frozen scene.

Even from this distance you could see how the berg sparkled from within, kerosene blue. And inside a shape suggested Zoë's body, stooped like a question mark. Ingrid believed she could see the tracery of Zoë's bones, the violet latticework and filigree of her nervous system. Ingrid imagined being sat on top of the berg with a flashlight, buffeted around the slippery top-surface by offshore winds, moving south through open seas. Releasing Zoë's body, they would enter the waves together. Not buried in Einar's garden turning to leather, worms roiling the earth about her.

Nobody ever thought about Einar Reed until now. He was just the polite, beet-faced fisherman who kept himself to himself, who sat in the Anchor bar sipping his single malt or chewing on a seal flipper burger, rarely looking up from his newspaper.

She tells herself this is not happening. Every morning she has been walking down to the jailhouse, hood pulled up against photographers, ignoring the barks from the press pack as Jon manhandled them out of her way.

Their relationship had not been sexual, she told the Rangers. It went deeper than that. Besides, it had nothing to do with the investigation what she and Einar had done and how many times. The truth was she would only reveal her body to Einar in slow stages, an inch more of flesh each time. In the end he seemed disinterested and told her he didn't mind. She knew she had insulted his dignity as only a woman could. She put it down to male pride, not to his being insane or a pedophile. She had wanted it to be slow, special, to control what couldn't be controlled.

Einar had spent days searching the sea caves around the island for Zoë's body, those secret places of eternal, echoing midnight. He obviously cared about her. She tried to recall the way he'd look at Zoë, her mind creating awful scenes she couldn't erase, and she wondered whether Einar's looks and attention were ever solicitous. She remembered one particular day, down by the harbor, when Zoë skipped along hugging Einar's arm, her smile on full beam, and Ingrid realized how much they had both needed a father in their lives.

It was my fault, Ingrid told herself, that Zoe didn't have one.

The scroll of waves mimicked her pulse, the ebb and flow dragging pebbles and sand. Jon's skin appeared pinkly translucent. He had something to say but he wouldn't meet her eyes. Every muscle and sinew within her began to tauten. The glacial wind filled the emptiness between them. It made her hum inside.

'Why didn't you contact me?'

Ingrid took a small step towards the waterline. 'When?'

'When you found out you were pregnant? When Zoë was born?'

There. He'd said it.

She wasn't dumb. A man who lived like he lived, among other men at sea for months. Of course every harbor was a stage, for another woman, for the theater of missing and empty promises. Jon knew Ingrid's address but she had received no letters over the past eleven years, no postcards.

'It sounds stupid, but I think I knew,' he said.

'Knew what?'

'The day I left. Knew you'd conceived. I *sensed* it.'

'Right.'

'I could feel it.' He put a glove to his chest. 'In here.'

Ingrid set her mouth in silent disbelief. So where were you, she thought, when Zoë ran into the house sobbing because she'd hurt herself? Or woke crying in the middle of the night with bad dreams? Were you the one to shush her to sleep, stroke her hair? No. You'd have been at sea, docked in other harbors, other women.

'You want to know the truth?' she asked. 'I feel like I'm lying in Zoë's grave. That I'm lying listening to the soil, the ice, waiting for her. Where is she, Jon? Tell me what you think, really. Please.'

'You haven't answered my question.'

'I keep thinking about that moment . . .'

His face a dark knot. 'What?'

'When the pain is so much you beg them to kill you.'

'Fuck, Ingrid . . .'

She walked away, down between the tide-lines and into the lumpy waves until the water was a heavy chill around her knees, so cold it burned; but she needed to feel something. The sea recoiled, embraced; inhaling, exhaling. Between these watery breaths: silence. In the silence waits inexorable death, final pause of breath. The island was a heart and the waves its liquid pulse.

She opened her mouth to shout Zoë's name, but then moved along the coastline towards the headland, sensing Jon's eyes upon her for a long time, but when she reached the part of the bay where the rocks moved into the water, she turned to find the beach was empty.

Closing her eyes, she saw Jon's lips and tongue mouthing a single word.

Colorful.

When it should always have been three.

SUDDENLY HE was there, face blood-flushed from stooping through the tight passageway. He stood with his back to the open door and gestured towards the stairs.

Zoë looked at him in disbelief.

'You're raising a stink,' he said. 'You need a bath. Get.'

She walked past him and felt his fingers spread between her shoulder blades. His hand was shaking and his nervousness made her feel safe. She counted twenty-five steps up into the garage above, sensing his gluey eyes watching her ass from behind. She was breathless. The heat took her by surprise.

Sunlight and air, the most brilliant dream.

INGRID FOUND the letter in her hallway. It must have been hand-delivered because all of her mail was redirected to the Rangers' Office. There was no stamp and her name was scrawled in a hand she didn't recognize. She unfolded the single-page letter, skipped to the bottom, stood reading, and then went through to the living room and read it again. She stared unfocused at the wall for a long time, surprised she wasn't surprised. Trying to imagine a young boy with Zoë's face, another family Jon had created but couldn't be bothered with. This man, she always knew, found it impossible to make attachments. Leaving for us both. Indeed. She read the last few lines.

I have no right to ask you to forgive me but this is what I wish. I will keep looking for our daughter. I will do everything I can. I just can't be here any longer. It is too painful. I am leaving for us both.

She turned, sensing a presence in the room. No one. But there was a smell, a stink of fish, bleach; the smell of the morning fish market. She pulled on her coat and wended her way up to Enchanted Lights. She needed the comfort of work.

'You chose me. You looked at me. You're the first person who ever *noticed* me.'

Her response was no response.

'I phoned your mom and asked her if she wanted you back. No, she said. Fucking keep her.'

Zoë laughed and the slap was a flat sound off the walls.

'No one else matters. It's just you and me now. Forget the world.'

As time progressed his story changed. He told her there had been a war and that they were the only people left on Earth, like Adam and Eve, starting over. She laughed at the idea, but when she saw the desert for the first time she half-believed him, and she would do anything to get back up those stairs, to peer through the parlor window into that alien, parallel world outside.

She wasn't sure how much time had elapsed until she saw the coydogs and how they had grown. She stepped towards them, opening her arms.

He made a noise and the dogs attacked.

INGRID WOKE convinced Zoë was climbing into bed with her.

'Zoë?'

She dashed through the house, turning on all the lights, looking behind doors.

Just that rotten smell filling the cottage.

She checked the windows were closed and then fell to her knees before the smoldering fire, her heavy breaths making the embers glow. She rubbed her hands over the heat telling herself Zoë had gone and was never coming home. She had to get on with her life and she was an idiot for thinking otherwise. When she sobbed it was just a dry, painful retch. She crawled on all fours, rolling her forehead against the rug, believing her organs would come out of her mouth, wishing she could push Zoë from inside of her again, start over.

She turned quickly, sensing that presence in the room. Listened, waited, exhaled. She considered taking another sleeping pill but sleep was becoming her enemy, her bed a place to twist and writhe.

Her mother kept visiting her dreams. She'd see the image

of her mother's favorite cardigan with the appliquéd pink and red flowers along the neckline, and then she'd see the figure of her mother stood on the Bay of Sotra, summoning the winds with a knotted length of fabric while Ingrid held a sputtering oil-lamp, giggling to herself. But in her dreams her mother always became a winged, underwater shadow, a bird flying in slow sea-time.

She walked back into her bedroom and stared at the space where Zoë's crib used to stand, and recalled listening to Zoë at night, panicking, thinking she'd stopped breathing. She would rush over to the crib and find Zoë staring up at her, chubby strawberries-and-cream face shining from beneath the coverlet, her expression asking, Will you protect me?

The one thing I'm meant to do and I failed.

First it was all about being fucked. Being pregnant made her feel self-satisfied and sexy, like only she knew how beautiful she was beneath her clothes, how powerful her lovemaking could be. She liked to trace her index finger from the base of her vagina to her navel. This was everything, this line, and it was the line that would grow darker and more pronounced as the first trimester progressed. She liked to go to bed early and hold herself, and, at nineteen years of age, she masturbated to orgasm for the very first time. But then her body began to rebel and she started vomiting; it told her: there is more than just one of you now.

Women in the town, strangers to her, would comment on her *glow*. The glow that was born out of nausea. She had been female all her life but only now did she realize womanhood was a covert world and being pregnant was her initiation. She hated those women's moist-eyed looks as her body bloomed and bloated. Her breath stank, her hair thickened and her skin thinned. She felt stuffed with child, replete with this alien life-form eating away inside of her like some ghastly parasite.

She wasn't even safe at home. Her mother sat on the bed beside her, stroking Ingrid's stomach. 'You're spreading our tree wide again. These branches inside, reaching back east to the motherland. It used to be custom to hide your pregnancy.'

'From who?'

'You can't see the most dangerous things in life. Here.' Her mother produced a small knife and slid it under Ingrid's pillow.

'Jesus, Mother. What now? Peerie folk?'

'Aye. And the Devil hisself.'

'Well I'm not hiding this baby from no one. Satan's agents, whoever.'

'There was no rainbow when he arrived? Jon, I mean.' Ingrid shrugged.

'You're carrying a girl.'

'That right?'

Her mother produced a small bone from her apron pocket. 'Sheep's condyle.' Three times she raised it into the air and dropped it into her lap, saying, '*Spå ben. Spå ben. Spå ben.*'

Ingrid sat up.

'There. You see.'

'What?'

'Hollow there.' She touched Ingrid's face. 'The three of us will be fine.'

During the next few months her mother performed secret rituals away from Ingrid's gaze, but Ingrid would find strange objects scattered around the house, lengths of knotted straw, flat stones with coins atop, bizarre arrangements of silverware.

Everything began to taste and smell different; the world was a new and horrible place that invaded her senses. Her body began to ache, blister, crack. This *thing* was pulling her outwards, downwards, and she wanted her body back, wanted her old life back. In a moment of weakness she asked her mother how late she could leave it. Her mother slapped her face. 'Don't even *think* such a thing.' She was in this whether she liked it or not. A single mom. The Gulber women gossiped about who the father could be. They loved the drama.

Then it was time for the scan and everything, in a single moment, changed. Zoë's heartbeat over her own, the rapid whoosh of new life, Zoë's movements in electronic, chlorophyll green, the sonic echo, the cyclic whoosh. Zoë's heartbeat a rapid, gelatinous pulse.

Her mother stroked her hair and wept while Ingrid's life turned inwards.

Ingrid's pregnancy shattered whatever had separated her and her mother in the past or had caused them to be at odds – it brought sweet unity. Her mother sat with her whispering words of encouragement, wiping salty sweat from her eyes as Ingrid screamed and cursed throughout the thirty-eight hours of labor.

'Everything you go through in life will just be a memory one day.'

This was, Ingrid believed, the best advice her mother had ever offered, and it brought her comfort now, picturing a time when Zoë would be back home. Whatever

Zoë had been through there would be a slow, but sure, healing.

'Everything you've been through, Zoë, will just be a memory one day.'

Her mother died suddenly of chronic nephritis. Ingrid went to the hospital, expecting to find her reacting well to the treatment, but the nurse greeted her with, 'I'm sorry.'

Ingrid entered her mother's room and filled the small hand basin with warm soapy water and then removed her mother's smock. She soaked and squeezed the sponge and cleaned her mother's body.

Her mother's nakedness was the only thing that felt real to her at that moment.

KEEP ON pleasing him, she told herself, it's the least you can do, because up those stairs was real air, real light, real space. She knew that he was evil and that begging him was pointless, it would get her nowhere, he'd enjoy it and if she tried to escape he'd find her and kill her and then he'd torture and murder Ingrid as well.

She believed him.

He began to shape her life with his lessons and demands and petty torments, and in the monotony of the routines she divined the patterns of his mood swings and began to anticipate the bitter moments, the violent moments, and the sweetest calm that often bloomed between them. At these moments you could mistake them for a man with his young wife, moving around each other in deferent silence.

Rangers on the island of Unnr released an official suspect last night in the search for Zoë Nielsen. The 43-year-old fisherman, Einar Reed, was first questioned by Rangers on Christmas Day, eleven weeks after Zoë vanished on her way to school. Unnr news agency quoted the Rangers as saying that after days of questioning they didn't have enough evidence to arrest Mr Reed. It is believed Mr Reed has a history of mental health problems and was reported to have had a relationship with the girl's mother, Ingrid Nielsen . . .

THERE WAS someone in the cottage with her.

'Hello?'

Again she found that she was entirely alone.

Outside she pitted against the cold, but at last the snow seemed to be hesitating. Yesterday flakes fell like feathers all day, behind which her face became a blank disc. She was losing weight, slowly becoming invisible. Being erased. She heard an airplane in the clouds above and imagined it to be flying south and wished she were on that plane. She would not go in to work today. She'd make a lap of the island, searching for red.

'Things will never be the same, they's all know about me.'

'Why didn't you tell me?'

'What, that I used to be wacko.'

'I would never have seen it like that. Everyone has problems. Everyone has dark times. I should know.'

Einar hesitated, looked at his feet. 'No one will ever trust me again. The newspapers. I can't even be *looking* at another child. So I'm leaving. It's the only thing I got left to do.'

'No, Ein. I need you here.'

'Aye, afore you did. But not when he turned up.'

She took his hand, surprised by the leatheriness of his touch. 'Don't leave.'

'I'm sorry, Ingrid, but I got to go.'

'I've ruined your life.'

'I'll write.'

'No you won't. You won't write.'

'I'll write.'

'You're all I have left.'

He put his arms around her, squeezed her once, and then left her standing on the doorstep, embracing empty space.

Every morning Ingrid woke in Zoë's bed, blinking up at the ceiling light, questioning whether it was true, that Zoë had gone. And every morning it was like being beaten up, grief a bully of the worst kind.

It took her a long time to catch her breath. She emerged confused, exhausted, slowly reassembling herself. She felt the cold stabbing quickly through her, upward through her mattress, watching her breath rise. She looked over towards her oil-heater and saw the sheet of paper lying on the floor. She lifted the black-and-white image to her face. Zoë *in utero*. The snapshot of the moment Ingrid's life turned inwards.

She traced a fingertip along the fine line of Zoë's upper skull, and the four white circles of knuckles against her mouth, thumb-sucking. The 'S' shape of Ingrid's womb-wall curving above.

He cleared his throat.

With his Hudson's Bay coat heaped upon his bones, he was like a silhouette against the roily gray of the doorway.

He wore a slouch on his head that might once have been green and from a buttonhole hung a small gold anchor. He was tall, dark-complexioned, forehead low and cheekbones high, and though she couldn't see the whites of his eyes she knew the color at the center was blue-steel. He rubbed his chin with a rasp and again she noticed how small his hands were, like a child's. Fingers soiled, shaking.

The smell that had been filling the cottage recently – it was his. Not the smell of the fish market but a sex smell; the smell of herself on Jon's cock, his hand on the back of her head, pushing it between his legs. Finish me off.

He looked directly at her. She said nothing.

His edges were blurred, smudged. He snuffled, wiping his nose on the back of his hand, blue-steel eyes fizzing.

Grief. Dirty old man. That hunter. That vagrant.

She asked, 'Where is she?'

Within his beard a smile unfurled.

She asked, 'What do you want from me?'

He stepped to one side, blurring himself, his coat scraping the floor.

He said, 'It's the living that haunt the dead.'

'What's that supposed to mean?'

She blinked. He was gone.

Night had fallen. The windows were dim squares.

In the lamplight he looked peaceful.

'There are clean sheets in the cupboard,' she said.

'I know.'

They smiled at each other.

She asked, 'Do you need anything else?'

He didn't answer.

She watched as he pulled objects from his bag: a pocketbook, torch, bottle.

She closed the bedroom door behind her and stood in the hallway, listening to him touch Zoë's things.

THE FIRST time Zoë saw his cold bright stare accompanied by a smile the captive suddenly became captivated. This was the moment she began to covet his attention and her past was silenced a little bit more. There were moments when he was gentle, he stroked her and made her promises about the future, about letting her free, calling her 'dearheart'. But she would always do something wrong. She grew weak, thin; her skin paled, tinged green, but she honed her mind until it was bright as a new pin, her imagination the tool to get her through this. Whittling time. Talking to herself. You can do this. You can. And then one day he opened the garage door to the outside world, that Edenic hell of desert cacti and shrub, of cerulean-blue that slid from the sky like wet paint. Like something in a fever dream.

It was May 5, 2000. Today would have been Zoë's eleventh birthday. It was also a Friday, the day of the week that Zoë was taken. Ingrid had been living this way for seven months, trying each day to remember the sound of Zoë's voice.

It was good to see the light coming back again, especially in the mornings after so many dark days, cold days, in-bed days. Ingrid had been awake for hours waiting for the dawn, waiting for grief to arrive, her only company. Soon the day will come, she told herself. And it did.

She was tired of lying in bed all day. She had grown thin. She had less than twenty dollars in her bank account. There were no letters to write this day. There was no one to write them to.

Jon did not return. She did not fall pregnant to him again as she'd planned.

She felt Zoë's absence from the world so completely. That feeling, that inner certainty, was all the proof she needed. She felt it in the very cells that Jon failed to fuse, divide. He left nothing but absence; it was all that she understood.

She threw open the curtains and a tingle of goose pimples scattered across her body. She selected her best dress from her wardrobe, the one she bought on the first anniversary of her mother's death. She had asked Red Bess to baby-sit that day, intending to go for a meal in a fancy restaurant on the mainland and stay in an expensive hotel overnight. Her mother would have loved that; she would have considered it decadent; the extravagance, the sweet selfishness of it. But the weather had other plans, and so she sat playing with Zoë as the sky-clapping thunder raged, trying not to feel the claustrophobia of the island contracting around her. This was a couple of years before Zoë decided she only liked herself. Not in a nasty way; she was just at that age when all children become mysterious, inward-looking; that age when they start inventing themselves, when receiving filial love is an exception and not the norm. She simply preferred the view from her bedroom window to that of her mother's face.

Ingrid pulled on a pair of tights, snapping the elastic, enjoying the feeling. She slipped on the only shoes she owned that you could safely call feminine and then applied a touch of make-up.

She opened the kitchen window whence the soft May sunshine would come. Outside, like a cliché of springtime, she heard a rhythmic thump above the cottage, the creak and cackle of geese on their homeward journey, white arrowheads driving north. It was the sound of the taut sky being worked upon, and Ingrid sensed the turn and tilt of the planet. A breeze folded into the kitchen, bringing with it a whiskey scent of brine, of peaty earth.

People kept looking in on her. Red Bess, of course, and Ranger Anika who called recently with a solemn-looking gentleman she introduced as 'the doctor' and Ingrid knew this meant 'psychiatrist'. She thought of poor Einar and wondered where he was. Maybe he was happy, making a new life on the mainland? She didn't blame Anika and the doctor for coming but she sat and talked non-stop because it was the only way to make them leave. She lost her dignity a long time ago but had never felt saner.

She considered the kitchen and its many objects, the history of them all, from her mother and father until now, the intimacy of these objects, their chronicle of touch.

After Jon left she had started to see herself as a stranger would, and as she began chopping vegetables she had a thought. It all seems so clear to me now, she thought. I've been looking at things the wrong way.

The water in the pan bubbled to a boil.

Such quiet and stillness in the moment. Fire crackling. Nothing moved in the room but the flames and Ingrid's pulse. But there she was again, the young girl dancing along the wall, skipping between the flickering shadows, humming.

Ingrid snapped herself from the reverie. Today was not for tears.

'Happy birthday,' she said, raising her glass into the air. But she couldn't swallow. She lowered her head, communing with her thoughts, then spat the wine back into the glass and walked through to Zoë's room where her clothes lay ironed and folded in neat little bundles on the bed. In the lane outside she took a final look back. Her blood home, her spiritual home, all it meant and contained, all that life, that absence. That death. She held her breath to listen: the sound of singing in the distance coming from the church.

His ice-cold hand in hers, they walked down towards Unstad Beach.

Ochre- and ash-colored sands, meadow of sad-eyed she-seals carrying pups, grown in the belly of the northern Atlantic, surfing in on the spring tide, the earth and moon and sun in alignment, drawing long waves right up to the grass line, 600 breaks an hour, banging, sucking, tide-bumping. The clouds above separated, spilling light down into the waves. Blinking, Ingrid watched the spray and fume roll in, white, nebulous.

Fingers stiff with cold she shrugged herself from his grip and walked down between the tide-lines where the sand had the color and firmness of asphalt, etched by waves and streams, strafed by snarls of tang. She bent to pick up large stones and placed them in her pockets. At the water's edge she glanced over her shoulder and though you never wave at sea there he stood, beckoning.

She mouthed the word. Father.

Too late.

She smelled the sea's depths; deep currents calling to her, a-murmur, deafening, and the sea began shifting its colors around like Jon's eyes. Without thought she removed her shoes and tights and stepped in, waves sucking holes beneath her feet, sand between her toes. She struggled for balance against the sea's momentum, a force sent from the other side of the world, the shock of the water so complete. Water lapped at her waist, a throb in her pelvis, tickling her breasts as she trod across rocks covered in clams, limpets, snails. Arms outstretched for balance, wrack twining her ankles, the water was already up to her neck when she found the point where the land plunged into the deep. Curling her toes around the lip of the drop-off, alone among the waves, sensing such freedom, her vision etched with wave-forms, she dropped into the overwhelming vertigo of the sea's depths.

Her earthly shadow swam away from her.

IT FELT as if her senses were being invaded out here; the destructive light and cloying heat; the perfumed breaths of desert flora; the maniacal laughter of grackles sequestered in the trees. Her limbs weren't used to so much exercise and she tottered like an old woman. The southern light's rise and fall, it was so confusing, disconcerting, and when she saw the vast landscape surrounding her in every direction she wanted to go back down to the room – she had started calling it her 'tomb'. But the tomb's silence and stillness were always within her; all she had to do, she found, was hold her breath and close her eyes.

With the rifle's glassy eye scrutinizing her every move, and the dogs trailing her, she took another tentative step out into the desert. Into the unknown.

RANGER ANIKA Jonsson sat on the sands of Unstad Beach in full uniform. A tear fell from the tip of her nose into the cap she held in her hands. Beside her feet the retreating tide had left in its wake the weed-covered corpse of Ingrid Nielsen. Across Ingrid's bloated face an eerie smile was set, an expression of enrapture. Her eyes were open, opaque, like the flesh of a mollusk. Behind Anika and Ingrid, arms folded across the hemisphere of her breasts, Red Bess stood, face set in anger.

Beyond the three women on the beach the distant hills of Asgard Fea loomed. The snow that still clung to the couloirs and talus slopes was slowly melting, running down over pebbles and rocks as if it were afraid, collecting in the streams that joined the rivers flowing out into the bay, where all waters combined with the North Atlantic sea.

2007

Coyote Plains, Arizona

The weeks leading up

to Zoë's escape

His eyes unbuttoned her.

She lifted the picture frame and rubbed the duster over the image of his mom, a gaunt woman in Levi's and rawhide jacket.

'She was real pretty,' Zoë said, inhaling his smell as she turned – the smell of greasewood bushes after the rains.

He leaned against the wainscoting. His lips were always open, spittle-wet; it lent his face a dim-witted look. His Stetson had left a ridge across his forehead like a pale sweatband.

'You got her eyes,' she said. 'I wish I could've met her.'

He examined her in great detail as she repositioned the frame and then lifted one of the white doilies, a knitted snowflake.

'That's enough,' he said. His desert drawl with a girlish lisp.

'Sir?'

'Pack your things away and get washed up.'

'Yessir.'

He didn't follow her.

She put the cleaning box back under the stairwell and

headed into the bathroom, leaving the door ajar. She could hear him moving about the house, his slippers flopping across the floorboards, the luffing sound of his jeans. The house was old, large, wooden, with flaking paint and loose window-panes and a noisy, corrugated roof. Every day there was a fresh coating of dust, mica from the desert outside, making the surfaces of the rooms sparkle.

After she cleaned he usually let her read in the parlor. The books belonged to his mom and they were the only things he let her take down to her room. Romances, he called them. He'd sit opposite to her, studying his manuals or fiddling with the rifle in his lap while she pretended not to observe. Sometimes he played records on the old portable Victrola. Country music. Women with wet voices. Men who sounded like they'd given up.

Often there were impromptu classes: Spelling, Grammar, Math, Cookery. But mainly he taught her about the local plants and wildlife, the two of them stood behind the parlor window as he pointed with blunt fingers, leaving greasy marks. He would tell her about the different names for the trees and shrubs and lizards and birds and then test her while they both stared out across that horizontal nothingness. Sometimes he brought plant specimens in and let her draw them.

But there were questions not to ask; about the island; about Ingrid. He'd glare and remove his belt. Send her down.

Tilting her face to the bathroom window, she felt a needle of pain as her pupils dilated. Between the cholla cacti outside, she could make out cloudbanks gathering in the distance, etched vividly against the blue. Searching for an airplane.

It would be easier, she often thought, if the world had stopped.

She washed her hands thoroughly and then cleaned and dried the basin with a towel. Without a trace.

He stood at the end of the hall and opened the kitchen door and waited for her to pass. She didn't see it at first; she looked around at the wood-burning stove and wicker furniture and the enormous mantel clock that she had never heard tick, its hands stuck permanently at 2:30 – the time, she imagined, she arrived at the house and her old life ended.

He gestured towards the kitchen table, covered by a battered oilcloth. In the center of the table a candle burned dimly.

'Happy birthday,' he said.

They had never celebrated her birthday before. Never had he asked her when it was. No Christmases, even. No tinsel or colored lights.

She walked towards the table where there was a small, circular cake, chocolate melting beneath the flame.

'You're eighteen today,' he lisped.

She felt her eyes widen.

She was ten when he took her, she knew this. So she had been here eight years if he was telling the truth. She thought it was longer.

'Thank you, sir.'

'Blow it out.'

'And make a wish?'

His eyes shone in the candlelight. He stroked his cheeks, stippled with the sink-holes of acne scars.

She leaned forward and blew and then folded her arms, watching the smoke rise towards the ceiling, thinking it would always be that date for her, the one she never got to write at the top of the page at school that morning: Friday October 8, 1999. Inscribed, instead, onto her brain.

He opened his mouth and inhaled a long, deep breath, holding it for a moment. She thought he was about to break into a rendition of 'Happy Birthday'. 'Here,' he sighed, passing her a bag. Inside were a sketchpad and a box of colored crayons. 'Do you like them?'

'Where'd you get them?'

He wiped saliva from the corners of his mouth. 'You'll find a dress in your room. I want you to wear it to dinner tonight.'

'Dinner?'

His hair caught on the stubble of his chin. 'I'll call you.'

'Yessir.'

'Be ready.' He paused.

'Yes?'

He licked his lips with the tip of his tongue. 'Never mind.'

She climbed the ladder to look at the dress spread across her bed. It was pink, plain; a school uniform. She pulled a face though she thought it was pretty. There was a grocery sack next to it; inside she found a make-up set, some perfume, and some pads for when she bled. She climbed back down the ladder and stood for a while, staring at the drawings of the outside world, tacked onto the walls.

She spent her free days exploring the surrounding land on foot, but he was always watching, stalking; the dry crush of a footstep; the glint of his riflescope. Wandering beneath the high cyanic sky, scattering lizards and birds as she filled her sketchbook with drawings of desert flora. He'd always refused to buy her a new sketchbook and so once the old one was filled she had to erase the drawings and start over again, creating ethereal palimpsests.

She sat at her desk, piled around its edges with the well-thumbed, old-fashioned romances, the *All Color Child's Encyclopedia* and a tatty *Practical Pocket Dictionary*. She peered up at the clock; the second-hand appeared jammed, a taunting flicker. The room stretched and squashed time, a second was sixty and sixty a thousand and a thousand one. She began drawing with the new crayons, multicolored barnacles and anemones, but stopped to count out the years on her fingers.

It would make today May 5, 2007.

Almost eight years.

She pulled the page from the sketchbook and tore it in half.

The screen door clattered behind him as he walked along the hall and entered Father's old bedroom. He checked the CCTV, watching her on the screen for a moment before using the remote locking device to secure the bunker door.

He went back outside to the pickup. Feet wide apart, he stared out at the battered sails of the defunct bore-hole and the browse-line on a long-dead thicket where cattle nibbled many years before. But there were no calves bawling today, just a cloud of insects droning around the dead deer, a mature, six-point Coues buck, its rear end covered in scat. He untied it from the flatbed and dragged it into the shed and hung it by its back legs and then rummaged through some drawers. Above him, on a long wooden shelf, sat large Heinz pickle jars full of bark scorpions and recluse spiders, bull and king snakes suspended in murky formaldehyde.

He found the knife and set about cutting the buck expertly from its chin, down along its stomach to its tail with a decisive stabbing motion. Its guts slapped onto the earthen floor. He put his bloodied fingers into his mouth and whistled.

The slat-ribbed dogs appeared in the doorway, ears pricked, tongues lolling.

'Good boys.'

She was dreaming of the North again, of that wet light, of giant hills decapitated by low grey cloud. Ingrid was searching for her, calling her name on moorland bluffs. Zoë tried to twist her tongue around the memory of a word, drooling onto her arm and the desktop. She woke to the harshness of the tiny room. She could remember little of the girl she used to be, but occasionally memories came back to her in the form of dreams and she would rush to draw the dream before it faded, folded inward. Because when you draw something you'll remember it forever.

So she drew the mountains and then tacked the page on the wall next to her bed, besides the drawing of snow falling out at sea and her sketchy map of the island. She tried to recall the feeling of rain on her skin and of a wind so fierce it stole the breath from your mouth. Nothing.

Eight years.

She wondered did Ingrid even think about her anymore?

'You got a few minutes to get ready,' his tinny voice through the speaker.

She rubbed her face and squinted at the clock.

'And I want you to use the make-up and perfume I got.'

She tried to remember Ingrid wearing make-up.

'Lickety-split,' he said. 'And do your pigtails.'

She washed her face and brushed her teeth and ran the

comb through her dusty-blonde hair. Then she undressed, folding her clothes neatly across the plastic chair. Naked, she looked over her shoulder and smiled towards the lens in the top right-hand corner of the room. Remote iris. She pulled on the dress and applied the make-up as best she could, feeling, she believed, like a woman from one of the romance novels. She rubbed the tingling scars on her right leg, the gnarled outlines of dogs' teeth.

The smell of food and fresh flowers was a sickly combination. Country music came from the Victrola. He was wearing his pale blue shirt and his usually lackluster brown hair had been pomaded and parted to one side. A smell came from him as he leaned down and kissed her cheek. 'Happy birthday.' Kerosene breath. He pulled out a chair for her.

'Thank you, sir.'

He served the fried squash with green chilies, boiled potatoes and sourdough bread and then opened two beers. He'd cooked his favorite meal for her and looked pleased with himself. She wondered what it meant.

He had a way of eating, of groaning with satisfaction while chewing, that irritated her deeply; and the way the tip of his nose wobbled; and the way he sucked and picked at his teeth when he'd finished. Moaning, clearing his throat. It hampered her enjoyment of every meal they shared.

When he was finished he pushed his plate away and leaned back in his chair, itching his crotch and then his neck. He hadn't shaved all that successfully, clumps of stubble remained along his neckline and beneath his ears – he should have asked her to do it – and the fine wrinkles around his eyes, she noticed, were full of desert dust.

She forced the last piece of potato down, looking up at the meat hooks hanging from the ceiling. She always thought they looked like children's fingers.

He drank his beer and stifled a belch.

She wanted to ask about the scars on his hands but he began to talk about the drought. 'There'll be rain tonight, but,' he said, his nasal voice almost a whisper, forcing her to listen closer than she'd like.

She said, 'You ever seen snow?'

He squinched his eyes at her, gunmetal grey, reflecting the world. 'Snowed real heavy last winter. But we don't get no honest winters here, not really.'

Her mouth formed a silent O; he smiled his asinine grin.

'Was she from here?'

'Who?'

'Your mom,' she said. 'From the desert?'

He leaned across the table and patted her arm with callused fingertips. Something appeared to be eating him; he chewed on it.

She lifted her hand into the air and heard Ingrid's voice as she began to recite the finger-naming song, 'Peedie Peedie, Paddy Luddy, Lady Whisle . . .'

He nipped and twisted the skin on her arm. She inhaled sharply but didn't flinch. They eyed each other.

'Quit that island shit,' he said.

She started repeating the song again.

'That mouth of yours.'

Her heart thudded hollowly as she continued.

He lurched and grabbed one of her pigtails, snapping her head back. Face above hers, eyes drilling, he stepped inside her and turned off the lights.

She smiled, and as he sat back down he gently passed a hand over one of her breasts, as if by accident.

'Touch me if you want to touch me,' she said.

He removed the small clasp knife from his pocket and she wondered if this was why he was being so nice to her. I will die tonight. She no longer cared. He'd be doing her a favor. She stood, shaking the feeling, and drifted past him. A small victory. She ran water into a glass and returned to her seat, his eyes upon her.

'Don't you like it?' He nodded at her glass of beer.

She shrugged.

He took the bottle and held it up to her cheek. 'The same color,' he said.

'What?'

'Your eyes. Bottle-green.'

The way he could be so sweet, the dizzying spin of his mood swings. She listened intently to the changes in his breathing, trying to divine his thoughts, what's next? She asked, 'You been reading my romances?'

He looked confused.

'We should have more music,' she said, lifting the hem of her skirt and opening her legs, keeping her eyes on his.

He looked at her askance, nodded.

'Then you can tell me more about your mom.' She leaned over and removed one of his cigarettes from the pack and shucked it between her teeth.

'Take that out your mouth'

She left it there, picking at the bread on her plate, making a small sourdough figure of him while he talked, no bigger than her smallest finger. She laughed through her nose.

'What?'

She spat the cigarette out. 'Nothing, sir.'

She ate his bread arms, bread legs, bread head, and got to her feet with a grunt.

'The dogs,' he deadpanned.

She saw his flies were open. 'Maybe I could go out tomorrow?' She grabbed her stomach, pinched a roll. 'I'm fat as a pig,' she said. 'Maybe I could go the other way tomorrow, in the other direction?' She pointed towards the front of the house, her hand shaking.

'You mean the road out of here? Yonway?'

She nodded. He laughed loud and long.

'Is that what you wished for?'

'What?'

'When you blew your candle out?'

She shrugged.

'They ain't nothing there anyways.'

'May I use the bathroom, sir?'

He closed his eyes dreamily. 'Use the one upstairs.'

She knew it meant he would follow.

She climbed the noisy wooden stairs and stopped outside Mom's room. Strictly out of bounds. But she looked in once: tattersall quilt, clutter of old furniture, faint smell of earth. She placed a hand on the cold doorknob but then continued down the hall.

He was dreaming of his mom again, calling out. Zoë had been lying awake for some time listening to the way he held his breath between snores, the way life seemed to pause. Desert thunder, flat reports like rifle shots, echoed across the flatlands, and the rain pitter-pattered on the tin roof, a smattering on the windowpane. It had been years since she'd heard rain like that and there was something comforting about the sound of it drumming against the roof and of being in bed beside Thurman, warm and safe. Then she realized what she'd just thought and the rain sounded, instead, like a punishment from God.

Coyotes called their queasy refrain. The dogs barked in response.

She climbed out of bed and pulled on his denim shirt that lay crumpled on the floor and walked over to the window. There, on the rain-blurred horizon, she saw it again: a dim glow, a speckle of light on the edge of the playa.

Ain't no star.

She drew the curtains and walked back over to the bed. On her pillow the smudges of her painted face. She climbed back in beside him and thought about the noises he made, a high keening, and sometimes she would mimic the sound, whining it back at him. She wondered why he always made her look down at him going inside and why, only sometimes, he could make it go hard and why that turned him so mean. He called it 'rubbing our uglies together'. And sometimes she would have to lie there with her mouth open while he sweated above her and spat into her open mouth. But when he was inside she was someplace else: back on the island, walking along the cliff-edge, and the sounds he made with her body, palpatory and wet, were the sounds of the ocean pushing against the earth.

She rolled onto her side, turning into darkness.

She wore Mom's battered straw bonnet and red-rimmed sunglasses. The air was thick, shimmering, and the dirt appeared luminous, white-hot. Already the thirst sucked her pores dry. She chugged from the canteen and wiped her mouth. 'A gallon a day,' he'd told her she'd need. 'Or else the buzzards will pick you clean.' The sun was so fierce the desert creatures were hiding, plant life retracting, and the counterpoint of insects that usually whined about her head was momentarily silenced. A few foraging chickens skittered and scratched in the yard as the skinny dogs stood watching her, panting.

He agreed to let her walk in the other direction, to follow the track along which he drove to and from the ranch. 'You'd be walking for weeks,' he said. He'd told her so many times: we're so, so far from anywhere.

The heat of the dirt burned through his mom's ill-fitting boots. He covered her exposed skin with sunscreen before she came out, but still her skin snickered. He took his time, breathing on her, rubbing the cream into the bruise on her forearm, his lips moist and parted.

Flakes of mica glimmered on the desert floor like fish scales. Unbidden she remembered a word from the island dialect. *Glimro*.

She slumped, dejection coloring her in.

'The desert is *glimro*.'

She shook the feeling and followed his tire tracks for a few yards and then cut into the creosote brush and mesquite. She expected to see buds of life encouraged by last night's thunderstorm, male rain impregnating the land, but everything was its usual desiccated self. Cacti maybe a little fatter-looking, and that unmistakable, heady perfume of sage brush on the air.

She followed a bellying fence along to a derelict railroad carriage. She wondered how it got there, and considered, yet again, that he was a liar. The sun-weathered carriage reflected the sunlight like aluminum and all of the windows were broken. She stepped in.

The carriage had been gutted, empty except for the flensed bones of a long-dead animal in one corner. She stood before a window; about fifty meters away there was a large Palo Verde tree she hadn't noticed before. It was perfectly enclosed, like a painting, within the wooden border of the broken window frame.

She stepped out and searched for him, seeing a glint in the shadows. She walked back across the track. Beneath the tree were two small, white crosses. One of the crosses was overgrown, snakeweed twining around its yoke, but the other cross was immaculate.

She traced the woman's name with her finger, the cool of the marble taking her by surprise.

Marny. Dear Mom.

There is no silence like sitting beside a grave and listening. A falling-asleep breeze pushed past her. She imagined standing with him in this very spot, comforting him, but she couldn't imagine him weeping. She rubbed her hand across the cool dirt of the grave and remembered sand dunes shifting beneath her bare feet, the manes of sea-surf in a wild black sea. Ingrid's voice on the wind, shouting at her.

A distant vibration made her stand and hold her breath. Someone was coming.

He ran his finger along the walnut stock of his rifle, a bolt action Nosler Custom, another gift to himself after he killed Father. He lifted the shadow-line cheekpiece to his face and felt the perfect weld of his jaw against the stock. He got her in his sights with a finger covering the trigger, set to a crisp three-pound let-off. She was standing in the center of the track, looking back towards the house. The riflescope's reticle was calibrated to provide 200–500 yard zeroes and he could see the look of caution on her face as she moved towards the Palo Verde tree.

He lowered the rifle, squinting into the light. The way sound comes before sight in the desert. Then he saw the cloud of dust and knew.

He looked for the girl. Stay put or haul ass. He watched the black vehicle approach through his riflescope, sun winking off the windscreen.

He whistled for the dogs.

She ran across the track and leapt back into the train carriage and curled up in a corner, breathing heavily into her arm. Where is he? There was a pain in her stomach. The dogs howled then stopped. Finally the car passed and the thick engine noise faded. Silence. Men's voices in the distance.

She recalled a conversation they'd had. 'I need to know that I can trust you,' he said, and she'd said, 'Of course you can.' 'Because if it came to an emergency, if anyone ever came and tried to take you away from me, I need to know.' 'You can trust me,' she said. 'Then undo your blouse,' he'd said.

Beside her, on the carriage floor, she noticed a strip of metal the length of her hand. Serrated, sharp-looking.

She pulled down her panties and peed.

The dogs moved in front of him as the black Hummer came to a halt, ethereal wings of dust engulfing the vehicle. He told the dogs to stay, resting the rifle on his hip. The passenger door opened and a man stepped out, wearing a suit, a Stetson and aviator sunglasses. Then the driver stepped out. Two O'odham Indians dressed identically with slow, Hollywood-white smiles.

Thurman walked down the steps. 'You're on private property,' he said, trying to lower his contralto voice, eyeing the two men from under his hat brim.

The men removed their sunglasses and squinted at each other for a moment. One of them opened a briefcase and offered Thurman a piece of paper.

'We'd like to talk to you about Coyote Plains.'

Zoë waited with the liquid sound of blood in her ears, counting time. When she peered out of the carriage he was standing there, rifle slung across his neck yokewise.

Hackles bristling, muzzles sniffing, the dogs circled.

She stood perfectly still.

'I tried to hide real good, sir. I did what you said.'

He propped the rifle against the carriage and kicked the dogs out of the way. Beneath his hat his face was dark, threatening. His shirt was open to the belly, small crucifix sparkling amid scribbled chest hair.

Shading her eyes, she saw the silhouette of his hand eclipsed against the sun. It hung in the air for a second, bunching slowly.

THURMAN SAT in his chair until the eastern sky began to lighten, listening to the sun's rays activate the landscape's overture through the open window, the simple beauty of the morning light fusing the bedroom air. Across his bed were the clothes he'd selected for the day — laid out, just like Mom used to when he was a boy. His boots stood at the foot of the bed and his wallet and silver crucifix chain were positioned neatly across the dresser top.

The house was silent below him.

Naked, he stood before the mirror, rubbing the knuckles of his right hand, still sore from where they connected with her skull.

He lifted his hand to his lips. Kissed it.

He liked the way the light caught his body, the way the breeze toyed with his chest and pubic hair. He had the physique of a seasoned ranch hand, tall and muscular with large pectorals, strong thighs and wide shoulders. His arms were thick and well defined but he was beginning to spread a little around the midsection. He sucked in his stomach and held his breath, puffing out his chest. He still looked good, he told himself, for a man of twenty-seven. He exhaled and considered doing a few sit-ups but turned fully, looking over his shoulder, flexing both butt cheeks and liking what he saw.

He picked up the hunting rifle and spread his feet, turning slightly, aiming at his reflection. Statue-still, he thought about the men in suits, all that money. His odd electrical jobs in town kept him ticking over, but only just.

And now he had to erase everything.

He thought about their nights cleaving together in the darkness, eye to eye, hipbone to hipbone. He went deep, bottom of her world. A place that was his alone.

He put on the silver crucifix chain and then dressed in a systematic way. Finally he pulled on his boots and buttoned his shirt and tucked it into his jeans and then combed his hair. He examined himself in the mirror, straightening his collar, moving his belt until the longhorn belt buckle was perfectly central. He cuffed his balls, jiggled his legs. Stared. Not a single face muscle moved until he winked at himself.

He headed downstairs and sat on Father's bed and looked at the coir rug and empty wooden shelves, the cracked mirror and the portable TV and tiny fridge full of Bud. He walked over to the desk, opened the locked drawer and took one of the letters from the top. Zoë's curly but meticulous handwriting:

You are my world. I long to make you as happy as you have made me. I am only happy when I am close to you. I love us. I love what we have together. I know I make mistakes but I will never break your heart. Thank you for rescuing me, for showing me a life of real love. I will never stop caring about you. When we are apart

you are all I think about. When we are together everything in the world is right. With you in my life I have
everything I want. In you I have all that I could ever
need.

I promise I will always love you.

xxx

Smiling, he folded the letter over and returned it to the
drawer, locking it. The lime-green lights of the modem shimmered. He clicked the keyboard until he found the file with
the images of her. Fingers undoing the buttons of his jeans.

Below, waiting for the light to come on, for her day to
begin. She scratched at the ceiling, gasped. The ventilator
rattled its weary duet and then stopped. She held her breath,
listened. I'm still alive. Turning onto her side, she lifted her
legs and gripped her ankles, rubbing her toes across the
ceiling. She imagined worms and underground creatures
beyond the wall, burrowing through the soil beside her
head. The claustrophobia passed as she climbed down the
ladder and shuffled over towards the toilet until she felt the
cold seat against her shins. She emptied herself knowing he
might, somehow, be watching.

This was her world.

He had rewritten her using food, water, light, air.

She had memory-dreams but she didn't remember the
girl she used to be or much about the day he took her.
Vaguely she remembered an argument with Ingrid and
walking to school through a storm and then waking up in
darkness alone, terrified, thinking she'd died, that this was
death. Which mostly it was. Life divided by who she was

then and what she is now. There were no calendars or newspapers or radio or TV up there, just the school uniform and red macintosh she was wearing the day it happened, hanging next to her bed, so small against her body now.

She pictured him moving about above her, thinking his thoughts, lifting objects and replacing them carefully, tongue flickering between spittled lips, checking certain drawers were locked.

Come down.

When she opened her eyes and closed her eyes there was no difference; she couldn't even see her hand in front of her face. I can't do this for another second. Thoughts like these increased in frequency, as did the mental asphyxiation, just like the first few weeks of her captivity when she tried to fight falling asleep, when she banged on the walls and screamed until she lost her voice and fatigue took her. She knew that she was underground, buried alive in her concrete coffin, her tomb.

The fear of going mad so much worse than the fear of death.

She heard her blood pumping through the vessels near her ears and thought it was the ventilator. No. She told herself don't react. Her stomach growled, fizzed, hunger curling her like burning paper. She wondered how much air she had left.

She sighed. She could do it. Outwait.

She fell asleep thinking about the shred of metal on the carriage floor.

He drove out to the cattle grid and tore down the sun-warped sign and erected the new one. VIOLATORS WILL BE PROSECUTED.

He considered replacing the locks on the gate but saw the gaps in the bellying fence and thought what's the point? He stared out across the playa with chrome eyes: palisades of mesquite posts forming a derelict corral; in the near-distance coulees shimmered like blood. A hawk's killy and stoop was the only movement or sound in the blue high, but he spotted something on the ridge of the far mesa. A figure on horseback. The rider appeared to scan the playa before moving out of sight.

He thought about the offer to buy the land. They told him how the company had been conducting exploration field trips in the area and how it was still rich in untapped mineral deposits. They mentioned the new technology but they didn't say the word itself. Copper. Gold. Oil. Uranium. Whatever. He knew nothing about environmental law and didn't give a damn about rehabilitation of the land once the mine was no longer viable. The men appeared to have everything covered. So much cash for a signature. He knew he could probably get more without a squeeze. He'd seen the new mining camps out towards the mountains but never thought anything of it. It could be a fresh start. Somewhere new.

Another girl.

Later that evening he drove out to the mesa. Staring down into the beams of the pickup's headlights, the vehicle lurched along the track, making the beers on the passenger seat clink. He parked on the ridge. Below, the town was a grid of lights reflected off the desert floor. He sensed her in the space behind him, a forty-minute journey back into the playa. He saw her Arctic-green eyes blinking, her fine-boned hands touching her throat. He cracked open a beer and swayed on his heels. Like a man about to start something.

*

Scanning behind sweaty eyelids, she saw the staircase out of there, lit in a blinding pane of light as she ascended through the doors and there he was, as always, proudly naked, smiling. She woke and lay blindly in the dark, eyes open. These dreams and memories, refracted and distorted, so Technicolor, so unreal.

Unaware of his presence in the room, she smelled the food, a smell so invasive she held her breath. The bolt on the door went *click* and the ventilator began to breathe with her, in unison, accompanied by the slow spread of light.

It was over.

She climbed down from her bed and ate on her hands and knees like an animal, looking up at the lens, but three mouthfuls left her full. She sobbed and then vomited. Ate. Vomited. Ate. Rested.

She struggled to stand, pressing her ear to the door, warm soft whorl against cold steel. She pictured the three sets of stair doors leading up there, away from her tomb. Craving his company, his touch. Hating herself for it.

Come down here.

He parked outside the Beal Bank and sat for a few minutes remembering these streets when he was a boy, the razzle-dazzle of the annual carnivals with their parades and floats and teams of bandsmen, the hee-hawing burros and vaqueros bucking their broncos to rapt applause. And he recalled the detonations from the now-defunct mines shaking the school building, soft rain of dust falling onto his head from the beams above.

Mom would always drive him to school; it gave her the opportunity to spend the morning traipsing around the antique shops along the main thoroughfare, a mile-long strip of brick buildings with false wooden fronts painted to look Oldworld. During class he would imagine her delicate fingers touching Italian wardrobes and grand pianos, ancient grandfather clocks and European porcelain. He hoped one day she'd buy something ridiculous, costly. The look on Father's face.

He recognized the attorney's Buick parked a few spaces down.

So they were already talking inside.

He slid a finger down the collar of his shirt, his gabardine suit making him sweat like a fat man. Beside him on the passenger seat the contract from the men in suits lay folded up. Mom wouldn't have to think twice. He'd make the request: the graves go untouched. Consecrated ground.

He placed the letter in his breast pocket, stepped out of the pickup and walked towards the bank.

DAYS LATER they ate eggs and beans together. The small things he did, like pouring the coffee and smiling without looking at her.

How much these things meant to her.

After breakfast they moved into the dim-lit parlor and he began to build a fire. The book she had been reading sat on the arm of a chair. She thumbed through until she found the dog-ear and sat pretending to read, sneaking looks at him while he handled the shotgun, ejecting, reloading shells into the magazine, cycling the action as she observed, took note.

White smoke snaked up the stove-pipe; the smell made her want to lie down.

He asked, 'You want to watch a movie tonight?'

'You got a television?'

He raised his brows.

'Since when?'

'It was Mom's. Small one. She liked to watch it in bed.' She thought about the grave. 'You mean Marny?'

He blinked at her, swallowed. Her heart thumped hollowly.

'What you say?'

She nodded towards the window and asked again, 'May I, sir?'

He had a distant look she could not deduce. He nodded. 'How long do I got?'

He wiped his lips with his thumb knuckle. 'Long as the sun's up.'

This meant nothing to her, for the southern sun always fell at such an alarming rate. Back home, midsummer, the sky would never reach full darkness, it would simply condense into a blue-black light, holding incomplete constellations with only the brightest stars making it through. And during the long winter months dawn would break at ten and dusk descend at three. It made no sense to her at first, the more equable southern seasons, the rapid swap of light. She thought Thurman was playing tricks on her, moving the hands on the clock in her tomb.

She stood in the middle of the track, squinting up at his bedroom window. She drew an invisible line towards where she saw the dim glow on the edge of the playa and moved in that direction, pausing beside the derelict carriage. The high-density light lathed the surrounding cacti to smooth green planes. Her skin felt cauterized.

She pictured the shred of metal on the carriage floor, but she could feel his eyes, feel him reading her mind. He was always inside, wearing her.

She stumbled away, between chiasma and four-wing salt-bush, until she found a rocky barranca winding through the playa. She followed its rim for a few minutes until a mark in the dirt made her stop and hold her breath.

Prints from a horse's hooves. The tracks led out towards

a grass swale. Instantly she remembered a small pony, wild-eyed and dirty, Ingrid encouraging her to mount it, the pony's staccato trots knocking the breath from her lungs. But he didn't own a horse.

Is somebody out there?

She thought she heard the dogs panting and turned but couldn't see the ranch house. The pain in her stomach returned; maybe he'd drugged her again.

A jackrabbit hopped from a bush in front of her making her heart clatter.

She headed back.

Fat and round, the carriage shimmered in the heat. She couldn't see him. She hummed to herself as she stepped inside and bent with a groan, picked up the shred of metal and slid it between her stomach and skirt.

The dogs stood together, ears pricked as she approached the house. They were becoming lazy. She imagined blood running dark from their necks and smiled.

They sat in the living room in front of the small television set. He observed her looking at the screen as though she didn't recognize what she was seeing, moving patterns of color and light she couldn't interpret, while inside his head he parsed the mechanics of what needed to be done and knew that he must burn her body at night. Smoke attracts attention. Tomorrow you die.

'You gone poisoned me,' she shouted, making him jump.

He sat upright and rubbed his face. 'You must've caught something.' As he lisped he felt like a small boy again. 'You're not used to the heat out there,' he added, thumbing over his shoulder.

'You *starve* me and then you *poison* me.'

He climbed out of the chair and went into the kitchen and brought her a glass of water, holding it a couple of inches from her nose.

'Drink this.'

She leaned back. 'No.'

'Drink it.'

'I'd rather die.'

She dashed from beneath him and out of the room. He sighed and put the water down and walked out onto the veranda where the dogs bristled and snarled.

'Go away,' she shouted into the dark.

He looked but there was nothing out there. He stepped in front of her, grabbing her arms.

'Don't send me down tonight,' she said. 'I'll do anything.'

She crept down the hall and tried the door to Mom's room, pausing to listen to him snore: a low epiglottal sound. She could still feel his fists in her scalp.

For some reason she remembered the day she first started bleeding, thinking she was dying, lying still and silent until he came down. It made no sense and she blamed the things he did to her.

Her eyes adjusted to the semi-darkness. The room smelled musty, sour. She stood for a moment looking at the large, tattersall-covered bed, imagining Marny propped up on pillows watching the small television set.

She tiptoed around the room, adrenalin scorching her stomach. Too scared, even, to switch on the light. But there was nothing in there that she could use.

She had to go back down to her tomb and get the shred

of metal, come back up here and whisper into his room. She imagined the brink of the jagged edge tearing at his throat. He'd asked her so many times: I'm six feet tall and 220 pounds, you don't seriously think you'd stand a chance?

Moonlight fell cold and silver through the window, illuminating a chest of drawers, across the top of which sat photo frames of differing sizes.

She walked on over.

Here was the only photograph without people: buildings with pitched roofs curving eastward around a harbor, eaves facing out towards the sea. She saw it and knew; something deep inside of her screamed this is your home, where you belong.

Where he took you from.

He found her side of the bed empty and with a painful clarity he knew exactly what he must do. He walked downstairs and into Father's old room and checked the screen.

The sound of her breathing filled the bunker.

'Dumb cunt.'

HE WATCHED from his bedroom window as the dogs began
trailing her into the mesquite. He left the rifle on his bed
and went downstairs and stood in the shade of the veranda,
wiping beneath his Stetson with a crusty kerchief. Finally
he walked across the yard and took the axe from the locked
cabinet in the shed and began chopping wood, carrying
armloads back to the garage door.

The sky had such bite today and the cholla shadows were
fingers trying to snatch her. The sound of him chop-chop-
ping in the distance continued. She turned; the dogs sat
beneath a white oak, licking, thumping their tails. Then they
stopped to watch as a Gila monster dragged its fat body
through the dirt beside them. Again she thought about
running, but she didn't want to suffer another dog attack.
She closed her eyes and held her breath and saw the image
of the harbor curving eastward in the photograph, secreted
beneath her bed sheets. Mind ice-clear, she knew that she
would never see her home again.

When he finished chopping he unbuttoned his shirt and

swabbed the sweat running down his ribs and pectorals. A minute later he was in Father's room, opening a bottle of Bud, frowning at the screen.

The staccato sound of his chopping ceased and for a moment everything seemed so simple. He came in earlier this morning; too early. There was no time to hide the shred of metal in her clothing. She would tell him she wanted to go back down there to get her drawing pad and crayons. She would get the metal and come back out here. She saw the image of herself slumped against the Palo Verde tree, blood emptying out over her.

No matter how hard he stared, there was something about the image of her room, particularly the arrangement of the sheets across her bed, that wasn't quite right. He stepped onto the balcony and saw the dogs beneath the oak, ears pricked, watching her. His breath became shallow as he quickly descended through the narrow passageway and into her tiny cell. Chartreuse of mold climbing the wall and the hot maw of her mingled smells – they always sickened him. He slid his hand beneath her bed covers and found the shred of metal, the photograph.

Slowly she walked past the dogs. One of them flashed its teeth but continued with its tongue. She headed back towards the house, around the large bundle of firewood. Here she turned and found the dogs weren't following. She opened her mouth to shout for him but caught her breath. She climbed the steps onto the veranda and walked through the kitchen and into the garage where the door to the bunker stairs stood open. She heard a noise coming from down there: Thurman clearing his throat. She stepped out of her boots.

He held the creased black-and-white image up to his face. The place where Mom grew up. The place where Zoë grew up. He sensed nothing. Just heard the bolt on the door, a *click* behind him.

How the walls closed in.

SHE STOOD for a while in the doorway to his father's old room, surprised by the sight of the home-made security system: the buttons, switches, microphone, laptop, the green screen of the CCTV mounted on the wooden desk. So this was where he watched her from, controlled her from. She'd always wondered what lay behind this door.

The dogs began their howling outside.

She walked over and touched the video-screen and pressed the switch at the base of the microphone. Breathed over it.

He flung himself towards the lens. 'Zoë?'

This was the first time he'd ever used her name and it stunned her, hearing it on his voice, from his lips. She wanted to ask, 'Who?'

She pushed a few buttons on the console and turned the dial; the screen went blank then came on again. She set the light in the cell to a slow flicker, his face there then not there as he continued saying her name. She saw herself in his face.

She stared at the laptop's keyboard, remembering the fights over the computer at school, and wished she'd paid more attention in class. She hit a key and it asked for a password, but she didn't even realize that the Internet existed and that this was her key out of here.

There was no telephone in the room. One of the two desk drawers was locked. Inside the opened drawer she found a bottle of baby oil and scrunched-up tissues. Lying beneath the desk was a gun, not his Nosler hunting rifle but the blue-barreled .12 gauge shotgun. She sat on the edge of the bed and laid the heavy gun across her lap.

The times he'd sat opposite her cleaning it, loading and reloading it, that grave expression on his face while she stole looks, soaking up and memorizing the minutiae of every hand movement, every curl of the wrist. With a groan she managed to cycle the action, glimpsing the cartridge sitting in the chamber. Staring at his hunting vest hanging from a peg behind the door, she wondered had he got his hunting rifle down there.

'Please, Zoë.'

She walked down the hall and the dogs barreled at the screen, white teeth snapping. She hefted the shotgun and rammed the end into their muzzles and screamed. Everything exploded in a blue-white light. The kick threw her against the wall. Blood hung in the air, a red mist suspended in a moment of death and beauty.

She peered through the hole in the screen. One of the dogs lay on the veranda, a chunk of its head missing. The other dog staggered in the yard where it fell onto its side, legs twitching in the dust, blood gathering like a deathly shadow. She watched it die before stepping onto the veranda and screaming, 'HELP ME,' but the sound of her voice belting out into that vast, perfect silence, terrified her.

*

The brilliance of the mid-afternoon sun was punishing. She reached through the open window and touched the downy eagle's feather hanging from the keys in the ignition and then climbed in. The pickup's dashboard was a mystery. She opened the glove compartment and found an opened envelope addressed to a Mr Thurman Hayes. Suddenly he had a name and the house had a name, but the initials of the state and the numerals of the zip code told her nothing. She licked her lips.

'Thurman. Thurman Hayes.'

She took a shell from his hunting vest, moved the laptop out of the way and after a few attempts she managed to reload. She placed the muzzle against the locked drawer, the butt against her hip, twisted her body away and pulled the trigger, wincing as dust filled the air. Tinge of wood smoke, camphor-scented. The drawer was shattered. There were papers on the floor and she recognized her handwriting. The times he used to handcuff her left wrist to the radiator and then turn it on full and dictate the letter, the glass of iced water waiting for her. The way he spelled out every letter of every word like she was dumb. She gathered up the sheets of paper and took them through to the parlor and set fire to them, her phony avowals curling in the grate.

She said, 'Thurman.'
He turned his head.
'Thurman.'
'You can call me that.'
'Oh, I'm calling you that.'
'That's real kind of you, Zoë.'

'I don't think you're in a position to be rude.'

Silence.

'The dogs,' she said.

'They can mind theirselves.'

'The dogs are dead.'

He rubbed his brow. She wondered was he crying.

'Where's the telephone?'

After a moment he said, 'Been no telephone for years.'

She removed her finger from the switch and watched him for a minute and then turned the dial full tilt. The tomb strobed.

She climbed the stairs to Mom's room and found a pair of cowboy boots with steel-tipped pointy toes and some ragged huaraches. She rummaged through a few drawers and came across a square jewelry box of black leather. She put on a ruby necklace and a silver bracelet, allowing herself to smile.

She crossed the landing to his room, relieved to discover his rifle lying across the unmade bed. But then she remembered the shred of metal down there, hidden under her bed sheets, and she knew at this moment that although she wanted to escape, she did not want Thurman to die.

She opened his wardrobe and took off her dress and pulled on a pair of old frontier pants and a checkered cowboy shirt. She rolled up the sleeves and pant bottoms and stood before the window, holding his rifle against her shoulder, scoping the flatlands.

Saw the distant mesa.

Saw cordilleras and mountaintops vaguely blue, far-off.

Saw the shape of what must be a building breaking a mote of horizon. But when she lowered the rifle and squinted all she saw was dirty white distance.

She searched both of the bedrooms but there was no telephone. The pain in her stomach returned. She dashed to the bathroom and strained.

He said, 'I told you.'

'You told me lots of things.'

'It said in the paper she'd killed herself. She didn't care for you.'

'Liar.'

'Suicide is for the selfish. The weak.'

'So all those times,' she said, 'you told me if I ran away you'd kill me and then you'd hunt Ingrid down and murder her as well . . . ?'

'There's nothing back there. You got everything you want here. Release me.'

'Why? What's in it for me? What's it worth?'

'You know I love you, dearheart. Like a wife. We belong together. You're the apple of my eye. We can close the bunker for good. Do it together.'

Maybe he was right. Maybe she was better off with him. There was nothing out there for her anymore. Maybe they could start to build a life. A life above.

'You promise you won't hurt me?'

He shook his head emphatically. 'No more. Never.'

She laughed raucously.

'The world is a bad, wicked place,' he said. 'You got no idea. I saved you from all of that. Don't you love me? Don't you want to marry me anymore?'

Silence was her response.

'If you had a boyfriend, he'd only want you for one thing. He'd want to fuck you and that's all he'd be interested in.

He'd pretend he likes you but all he wants is to fuck you
until he's bored and then he'll dump you and move on to
the next girl. And you'd be all on your own again, and what
would you do then, huh? You'd want to come back to me,
that's what. We can start a family. Haven't you always wanted
a baby of your own?'

She thought: And what if it's a girl?

He moved to the far side of the room and sat with his
back against the wall.

'It's you that's weak,' she said. 'Ingrid's alive and you're
a liar.'

He was crying.

Everything stopped.

It was a real sobbing jag, like he was trying to expose his
soul, like he cared a whit. But seeing this emotion for the
very first time, in a man she knew so well, created this
feeling inside her – a twisting, wringing, yearning.

She hated him for it.

'Thurman?'

Silence.

'You hungry, Thurman?'

Slowly he raised his head. A pathetic, lisped, 'Yes.'

She went to the kitchen and fried the squash and chilies
with a tat of butter in the black skillet. She carried the plate
through the kitchen's side door and into the garage and ate
the food on the crate in front of the ventilation shaft. She
ate quickly and almost finished the food before she began
to gag. She put her mouth to the griddled hole and felt the
suck of the ventilator against her lips, laughing down towards
him as loud as she could.

*

Hanging over a rung of the ladder that led up to her bed was the school uniform she wore the day he took her, her name sewn into the collar. She was so affectionate then. Innocent. Generous. So gentle and warm. He wished they didn't have to change. He remembered how her thighs smelled like warm butter. Her whole body in full light was his, from in front, behind, below, above, lying on her belly or on her back, opening her up like a flower whenever he chose, which was often. That was before she learned how to be naked in front of him and things began to change.

He touched the fabric and then sniffed his fingers. He pulled her bed sheets towards him, breathed them in. He held himself, staring at her drawings on the wall. How long has it been?

He hunched in the corner, shielding his eyes from the flickering light. The craving for a cigarette passed but the scars on his hands began to itch; his past was closer than he thought.

It was the day after Christmas and Father was out in the paddock at dawn. Mom was stood at the window, watching Father move between cattle cropping. 'Let's go for a drive,' she said. Two hours later they left the highway and headed out towards Mount Misery. They walked all day and didn't see another soul and were almost back at the pickup when Mom grabbed his arm. At the end of the track a mountain lion stood sideways on, a pheasant in its mouth, its yellow lantern eyes holding them both like Father's silences. Thurman stepped between Mom and the lion, raising the .22 caliber air pistol to his shoulder, useless for anything other than plinking cans. 'Don't, Thurmy,' was all she said. They watched it move away; Mom looked hypnotized. The blood rose in him and he ran after the lion into the bush, falling down a steep arroyo and landing on a broken bottle. She made him promise not to say anything to Father about the lion, but Father beat him when he saw the bandages. Thurman ran down to the bunker and locked himself away. It was a place where no one could see his pain. And now he was back here again.

He couldn't let her go wandering across the land. What if she died out there?

He would starve to death.

COYOTES BEGAN their high keening through the desert. She pictured them slinking from bush to bush in that limitless, horizontal darkness, trailed by bobcats and foxes, fur liquid-looking in the moonlight as they followed the scent of the dead dogs.

She went back into Father's room and watched the light flashing in her tomb. He hadn't moved for a long time. She found it hard to believe. This high feeling in her chest: trapped between fear and excitement, between the urge to escape and the fear of what will happen, the terror of *out there*, and all of his macho warnings came back to her, about how she would die so quickly out in the desert. She was free but trapped again.

She scrutinized him, her face close to the screen. She tried typing a few words into the laptop and then turned the dial until the light remained constant.

His reaction was no reaction.

Her reflection in the cracked mirror. She ran her fingers through her knotted hair, hair that he never let her cut. She went through to the kitchen and found a small pair of scissors and tied her hair back in a tight ponytail and hacked a ragged bob. She stood for a minute looking at the hair on the kitchen floor and then went back into Father's room and lay on the bed, observing him.

She lifted his sweat-stained Stetson off the hook and walked out onto the veranda, staring at the large pile of firewood, wondering what it was for? A buzzard lifted raggedly into the dawn sky and she noticed that a trail of blood leading into the desert was all that was left of the dogs, dragged out there by God knows what.

She squinted at the pickup, running through the memory again, of someone driving, a hand moving from steering wheel to shift.

She collected eggs from the coop, shit-streaked and warm in her palms, and cooked herself some breakfast. She expected him to walk through the door at any moment, for them to eat together and chat, for him to follow her around. Hearing her own sounds, her staggered breaths and foot-falls, the house felt eerily hollow, lonesome, like without him she didn't even exist.

She filled two canteens with water and then stood watching him in her tomb, blinking back her emotions. She ran from the house and climbed into the pickup and studied the pedals and dashboard before turning the engine over and ramming the shift into gear. The pickup coughed and jerked, but she was moving, engine screaming. She sat on the tip of the seat, pressing the gas to the floor, steering the vehicle away from eight years of life with him.

She turned the keys again. Nothing. Dirty smoke curled from the hood. The temperature in the pickup was unbearable, as was the rawness of her hands. She popped the studs of her shirt and chugged from the canteen and stepped out. Above, the sky was almost colorless in its acetylene burn. A surge of nausea hit her and she vomited onto the front wheel arch. She walked towards the pathetic shade of a tree she didn't know the name of, clutching her stomach and cussing herself for forgetting a hat and sunscreen. As if conscious of this, a pair of jays mocked her in the branches above. The tree stood twisted, pointing towards the direction of the buildings she spied through the riflescope, egging her on.

She observed the surrounding country, wondering how far she had come and how far she had yet to travel. She knew the desert could kill her, remembering Thurman's hymn again: you'll need a gallon of water a day, and the night time will freeze your tokus off.

She rubbed her eyes with the heels of her hands, trying to erase the memory muscling into her head: how Thurman once held her in the parlor and for a second they moved together in a slow kind of dance, how she forgot where she was, and how love bloomed hotly between them.

She climbed up into the lap of a low branch and the birds flew off. From this raised vantage point the landscape filled her with awe. Behind her, in the distance, she could make out the roof of the ranch house. She climbed back down, collected the canteens from the pickup and followed the tire tracks back.

THE PILLOW was cold and damp, but her shaking had stopped. She could smell him on the sheets, a waxen, animal smell. Again she recalled being huddled against his naked body; the mole on his left buttock and scar on his inner thigh; the way one of his nipples was folded over like it had been shot through with an arrowpoint. The wispy halo of hair snaking around his coccyx. His earthy, bitter taste. Him, down there, thinking his thoughts.

How the tables had turned.

She sat up and finished the last of the water from the canteen, the skin on her face, hands and neck scoured raw. Insect bites tingled like they were beginning to fester. She imagined shedding her skin like a snake.

She climbed from the bed and stood before the window and something about her faint reflection, her ghostly expression, reminded her of him.

She ran herself a hot bath and climbed into the tub, inhaling through gritted teeth, hating the magnifying effect of the water on her body, her dimpled stomach, thighs, arms, wondering what girls her age should look like. She lifted a breast and let it flop into the water. Blisters stippled the sunburn on her fingers, the same color as her nipples, the color and texture of raspberries.

'Dumb bitch,' she said, mimicking his voice.

The green and black of the screen made him look haggard. She rubbed the cream into her forehead, Aloe Soother with Jewelweed & Yucca.

'Ain't but one sure-fire way out of here,' he said. 'Here's what you need to do, and you'll be 100 percent safe.'

She waited a few seconds and then pressed the switch. 'Go on.'

'There are four doors.'

'Er, I know.'

'The fourth, the final door, being the door to this room.'

She sighed. 'Yep.'

'And the doors only open from the outside. From your side.'

'A-huh.'

'So leave the food on the steps between the third and fourth door and close the third behind you. When you get back to the room you can release the fourth door with the button on the console, and I can collect the food and bring it back in here to eat.'

The dark sockets of his eyes.

'And you'll tell me the way out of here?'

'Yes.'

'Because the sooner I find someone, the sooner *you'll* be found.'

'You won't let me starve, Zoë. I know you. You're a good person.'

She eyed the shotgun and rifle.

'Tell me which direction to go and I'll free you now.'

He laughed. 'Don't you trust me, Zoë?'

She walked around the room in a full circle, running her fingers through the peculiar feeling of her short hair, not knowing that these would be the last words she would ever hear him speak.

Adrenalin searing her temples, her stomach felt like it was full of acid. She laid the tray on the step and gently pressed her ear to the door and then snorted a glob of phlegm onto his food before climbing the steps back up.

The screen was a blizzard of pixels. She could hear him eating. She pressed the remote locking device. Nothing happened.

'What's happened to the camera?'

The eating noise continued. Her stomach tightened.

'What you gone done, Thurman?'

The device glowed red, green, red.

She heard a chipping noise and couldn't believe how dumb she'd been.

'I'm gonna be waiting,' she said, 'and I'm gonna shoot your fucking ass off.'

She jolted herself awake and rubbed her neck. A sound came from behind the door. She grabbed the shotgun and dashed back up the steps and read from the gloaming light in the hallway that nightfall was near. It's now or never, she told herself, but a wave of nausea broke over her and she ran to the bathroom and strained. A meaty, ferric smell; a smattering of blood in the toilet bowl. She cleaned herself and folded a wad of tissue paper into her panties.

Back in his father's room a light flashed on the console but she didn't know what it meant. Then she heard a distant vibration. The sickness in her stomach turned to fear.

An engine noise.

HE RESTED on the step and rubbed his wrist, thinking about the two crosses beneath the Palo Verde tree, graves and roots and him down here, dark and deep.

The two bodies.

Mom would show him photographs and talk about her childhood on the island in Canada, about a family and a country he had never known. Don't leave me here. He recalled her obsession with the phases of the moon, the lunar calendar she kept on the wall. The two of them playing dominoes and cards or snagging catfish in the old creek, long since dried up, with lines weighted with shot. A childhood of everlasting summers, helping her cook while she sipped her favorite tipple of pomegranate sloe gin and preparing the feast after the October cattle auction.

Her raised finger, wan smile: death-bed farewell.

He shredded Zoë's pillowcase into strips and wrapped them around the end of the metal for a makeshift handle. He almost admired her ingenuity, wondering what she had planned to do with the metal. He chipped away at the concrete for another twenty minutes until his hand cramped and then he pulled down her mattress and lay there and within a minute he was asleep and dreaming the memory: he was back on the island, rainy streets in black-and-white, the harbor wall slimy with diesel-stained sea-wrack, the girl wandering alone in the rain. If she looks at me. If she looks.

She stood in the darkness behind the door, cradling the shotgun to her chest. The car horn blew a few times then the engine cut. In the first few days of her imprisonment she was never sure if Thurman was alone. She thought there were two men, maybe more. Somehow Thurman had contacted them. They're here to kill me. The men's voices grew nearer; she breathed through her mouth.

Cumbersome gaits ascended the steps, clomping the wood of the veranda.

A man's voice: 'This one?'

A grunt. 'A-huh.'

'Anyone home?' The screen rattled and a man shouted Thurman's name.

She pressed her back against the wall, certain they could hear her heartbeat.

The door opened an inch and she saw a man's hand, broad-leafed against the black material of the screen. A large, gold ring.

'Don't like this. Not one bit.'

She smelled cigar smoke, earthy and thick. She thought about the broken-down pickup in the track and the dried dogs' blood beneath their feet.

Their footsteps led away down the veranda. She heard arguing, hushed tones, one voice rising above the other, but she couldn't make out the words. There was a terrible minute of silence before the engine started and they circled the house and drove into the distance.

She waited for a long time before going outside and walking up the track, shotgun poised. She stopped beside the Palo Verde tree, two marble crosses lit from behind in the beaten-copper dusk.

She took a bag from his room and began to pack for both the cold of the night and the heat of the day, wondering how far she could walk in the next few hours, pushing the thought of rattlesnakes from her head, trying to remember what he'd said about their only liking dark places. But what does that mean at night? After she packed the last of the food she went to the bathroom again. Nothing. Just the feeling that her body missed him.

She took the shotgun and the hunting vest from Father's room.

The chipping sound had ceased. The screen was totally blank.

Bag on one shoulder, shotgun across the other, she finally left the ranch house. Above, the blanket of stars reminded her of the enormity of the passage ahead, but she was playing that inner newsreel in her head, the one she knew so well: Zoë Nielsen's incredible escape.

She turned on the flashlight and stepped into the beam.

THE BROKEN-down pickup in the middle of the track. She tried the key in the ignition but the engine was dead. With her back to the pickup, she turned off the flashlight. The stars pressed down upon her. She flicked the light back on and walked for another minute before a searing spasm cut her in half, the bag and shotgun falling by her side, the beam illuminating a bush.

Inflows of pain. Fiery waves.

She tried to stand but buckled. Rocking, swaying on her hands and knees, it felt like she was on a boat. She began to howl but the pain stopped. She managed to stand and take down her jeans and shine the beam between her legs and try cleaning the liquid away. Got to keep walking, she told herself, but the pain cracked her in two again. She wanted to be below, down in her tomb, dancing with Thurman in the parlor, for things to be as they were, wishing she'd never locked him in the bunker at all. It came again.

Arching her back in the moonlight, her insides began to move. Something was sliding downwards, her muscles contracting around it, trying to stop it, hold on to it, but it kept coming down. 'Thurman!'

Hot. Thick. Muscular.

*

She shone the circle of light over it, dark lump in a mess of blood, immobile. Gnarled caul, nubs of limbs. Barely human form. She heaved then held her breath and closed her eyes, but the sound grew from behind her: stalking foot-falls. She dug her hands into the warm earth and covered the dead fetus with dirt. The blood between her legs was already starting to turn cold. She tried to still her breath for someone was stepping nearer. She heard the snort of a horse, dirt churned beneath hooves, the clink of a harness. She fired the shotgun towards the sound.

Rapid thump of hooves moving away.

She staggered away into the desert night. The weepy, exhausted, lustful craving for Thurman. Moon dragging her onwards like the tide.

THE OLD Indian woman followed Zoë's spoor back towards the ranch. She stopped occasionally to study cleat marks in the caliche; Zoë's story etched, how she had been dragging her feet and was in so much pain and the boots were way too big for her. The aerial spoor where Zoë had trampled through bush, blood spots.

The horse was edgy. Two female coyotes were in the track, sniffing, eyeing the figure on horseback. They stood their ground before slinking into the darkness to rejoin their pack.

There was a large amount of blood here.

The woman leaned back in her saddle cantle, thinking.

Her iodine skin was reflected in the flashlight as she dug, until her fingers touched warm flesh. She wasn't sure what she'd been seeing these past few weeks, scouring the edge of the reservation: the man with his rifle; the girl harried by dogs; and then the girl taking a pot shot at her when all she was trying to do was help. It was white man's business, but she couldn't leave this out here for the coyotes. It was no good, she would have to call the sheriff's office.

She took the blanket from her saddle and wrapped up the fetus, chanting a blessing to calm the departed spirit.

COYOTES YIPPING, encroaching. Zoë thought about them eating the bloodied flesh that came from her. She held her stomach, crying with pain, shining light onto a bush. At times an insect or moth spiraled into the beam. There was a sharp pang in the air, the crunch of windblown dirt in her teeth. Her stomach made deep quacking sounds between the crash and wallop of her heart. She heard the distant snort of javelinas and imagined it was a cough.

'Thurman?'

She realized she was hopelessly lost. She thought about the strange-sounding animals he'd made her eat over the years – kangaroo rats, opossums, porcupines – and she told herself she'd get through this maw snailing her brain. Save the food for later, she told herself. Her boots kept filling with dirt and the dirt grated against her blisters. She knew she should shine the light between her legs but she was scared of what she'd find. So she continued struggling forwards, towards what she didn't know, stumbling between sharp bushes. Gotta keep moving.

A sudden flash of sheet lightning on the horizon. No sound. Eerie spectacle.

In the early days she had believed she had been cast into the Underworld like some mythical island hogboon or troll and that it was Ingrid that had sent her there. The childhood terrors of Ingrid's tales, the horror of dark materials, unseen, moving beneath your feet, seeping through you. The boulders around the island, they all had names and a narrative, usually to aid those at sea in bad weather, and she believed she had been turned into one of these rocks. Or maybe she was Thurman's ogress, his *gyrekarling*. Standing lost in the desert, squinting up into the creamy wheel of stars, she thought the island must lie someplace above, beyond.

Coyotes cackled into the night, serenading the moon.

Her mind was sticking, pausing, playing images back vivid as videotape. Freeze-frame of her standing outside the cottage, looking down the glebe, feeling the roughly hewn land of rock and turf around her. Being taught at school about the words that cloak everything but she already knew them by a different name. She wore that cloak like she wore her silences. Skin-like.

This was the moment she had dreamed of since she found herself cast below, those first few weeks of eternal midnight, waiting for Thurman to come. This didn't feel like a happy ending; this felt like the beginning of the end. I will die this night. Thoughts like these smothering her, making her want to turn back, coupled with this feeling of being hunted. Ingrid must think she's dead anyway, taken forever. There was nothing to focus upon except her fear and pain, of being out here bleeding in the desert night alone, of that thing that just came from inside of her.

If you ever try to escape I'll kill you.

She stopped and turned, watching a tarantula tiptoeing through the circle of flashlight. Lightning flared close then moved away, blue and silent in the night, across this other-worldly landscape of fear. She drank from the canteen thinking it will be worse if he catches her. She should offer herself to him, gain his affections, forgiveness. She knew how. And so she began retracing her steps, believing she was heading back to him. Back to her tomb.

Beneath her boots the gravel made a noise akin to glacial moraine. Her whole body shivered. She zippered Thurman's hunting vest and blew into her hands. She had been drag-ging her feet for over an hour, though it felt like longer, unseen insects taking bites out of her. She pulled her trousers down, crouched and peed, but when the liquid came it burned like acid and she moaned deeply. When she stood up she saw the distant lights of what she believed was the ranch house and began to run.

But the ground fell away beneath her.

Tumbling down a steep arroyo, shotgun and flashlight and bag scattered, she plunged heavily through crucifixion thorn shredding her like blades, coming to an abrupt stop punc-tuated by a scream.

She had been spined by a cactus, a fishhook running deep and clear out of her scalp. Breath fogging the air, spirit rising out of her, a trickle of blood ran into her eyelashes, the shallowest of pulsebeats in her neck. Harried in her mind by rattlesnakes and scorpions, she tried to move, to free herself, but the fiery spine pinned her to the ground. All she could do was blink, the cold glitter of adrenalin in her eyes.

Close by, a lone lynx lifted his nose to the moon.

There were unseen things in the air above her and she was minutely conscious of their swooping flight, the sound of cicadas wadding her ears, or maybe the high chirrups of desert bats. There was a flaring in her skull, her eyes dipping in and out of consciousness. Slowly she brought her legs up to her chest, blood pooling in her right eye, and unconsciousness snapped her out.

Flies covering her, making her appear jewel-encrusted.

She jerked awake, right eye clotted shut. Through her left eye she saw a dark figure moving through the beam of flashlight, lynx with piss-colored eyes, snub snout sniffing the ground, brindled fur moving along its ribcage. She held her breath. Played dead. He blinked, smiled. It was Thurman. He'd come to take her back. She closed her eyes, awaiting death, and felt the stillness of the tomb.

GRIPPING HIS right hand with his left, blood seeping between his fingers as he climbed the stairs, he called again, 'Zoë?' He saw the hole in the screen door and the black trail of blood across the veranda and chunks of fur-covered flesh and knew the dogs were dead. 'Zoë!' He searched his room and then Mom's room; one glance told him things had been moved and that she had the shotgun, but still he roved the house like he was bulletproof.

In the bathroom he took a leak and then laved his hands, all the while shouting into the silence of the house about what he was going to do to her, snap her like a twig if she didn't come out. 'Can still save yourself, if . . .'

Pinkish blood swilled the plughole. He glared at his reflection and saw Father staring back. He opened the cabinet and removed disinfectant and gauze and administered to his shaking hand.

He checked the rooms again. Empty. The house was so quiet he could hear his pulsebeats and the silence spoke to him: it said he was as good as a dead man.

He switched off the light and peered through his bedroom window. A gibbous moon bathed the landscape silver. He tried to remember where he parked the pickup; that's when he spotted the headlights coming across the land and he knew.

He took the stairs two at a time and went into the parlor and moved the coat stand to the edge of the window, re-arranging his greatcoat and Stetson into the semblance of a figure, and then he ran into the night.

He could feel the weight and power and position of his heart as it hammered in his chest, crouching behind the bush, watching the lights of four police cruisers approach the ranch house, engine noises growing nearer, churning the dirt. No sirens. They's never gonna get you. Dust filled the headlights as the units braked. Even the coyotes were listening. Men's voices.

He looked up.

Stars scattered like gooseflesh across the night, revealing their patterns to him.

The troopers moved to the front three cruisers. Thurman squinched his eyes at the rear unit, an Impala parked up the track on its own, dome light on, doors open wide, no one in there. Praying it wasn't on runlock.

Slowly he shuffled back into the darkness and dashed to the next shadow, cussing the light of the moon. Breathing. Waiting. Watching. Pale desert djinn hopping from creosote to bur sage.

He reversed at speed, reopening the wound on his hand as he span the Impala around. Muzzleflash; the back window shattered. He ducked, steering into the barrial, shots caroming off stones as he shifted into second, engine blaring, minutely aware of the bullets passing the vehicle at the speed of sound. The warmth of the seat beneath him, and the smell of the state trooper's breath, disgusted him. He passed the derelict railway carriage searching for the shape of her. Someplace not here. The remaining units would follow his tracks but so what, he knew this country, this was his country. He looked in the rear-view as they began to twirl their lights. Shots continued. Aiming for the tires, he thought. No. They think you're armed. He reached into the glove box hoping to find the key for the firearm locker. Nothing. He flicked off the dome light and hit the siren for a second, the red light of the single beacon bathed the passing land-scape and he smiled briefly, a boy fulfilling a dream. The tires kept hitting ruts and leaving the earth, engine howling in lieu of tread, tossing him up out of his seat, the cruiser's underside crunching on rocks.

Zoë GASPED herself awake. The cold ground gnawed her bones. She was sure she heard dogs barking. She inhaled and clenched her fists, releasing a low groan as she pushed her head forwards, pulling her scalp free from the spine, screaming into the night on all fours, swooning with pain.

She crawled up to the flashlight, collected the bag and shotgun and then shone the beam around, but there were no paw prints running towards the cactus where she'd lain. Out of the steep arroyo she struggled to her feet, warm blood running between her shoulder blades.

Scanning the dark landscape 360 degrees, looking for guidance, she found she could see more with the flashlight switched off. The horizon appeared to flutter and flicker, producing a sensation that she was floating. She touched her skull, scalp raised and flensed where the spine went through. She wiped her hand on her pants and then snapped off a creosote branch and scratched a word into the dirt. Sorry.

SPEEDING PAST the old telephone trail where Father taught him how to shoot, he was out on the edge of the land where mesquite posts held rusted remnants of wire and the Impala passed through them effortlessly with the smallest of clicks against the hood. He hit the blacktop with a loud thrum, instant thrust of tires gripping asphalt.

If I die will Father be there?

His hands trembled, the adrenalin in his veins forcing the squawk of the radio into silence. All he heard was his breathing filling the quiet of the cab, the hysterical hitch to it. He stared into the road, power-poles strobing his eye corner, making him glance sideways: a large yellow dog limping across the apron of an empty gas station beneath many-colored banners. He absorbed this scene in an instant, just as he did the units in the rear-view joining the highway behind him. He goosed the Impala as fast as it could go, thinking, Will Father be on the other side, waiting?

He parsed the workings of the situation, of whether they'd found her or discovered the bunker and security system, pacing the maze in his head, the night air rustling through the open window, speaking of things supernatural. He never thought it would end like this. The cruisers in his rear-view were shimmering. He checked his speed, needle dialing the hundred mark.

He would see the headlights of the approaching vehicle but wouldn't distinguish the roof lights at red-blue alert from those in his rear-view. He would feel what he thought was an insect bite above his left ear but wouldn't see the perfect, dime-sized hole in the windshield. By the time he'd raised his hand to his skull the cruiser was veering into a sandy berm and slowly lifting, flipping onto its side like something in a dream.

He made guttural sounds, lying twisted on his side in the roof of the cab.

Surprised. Shivering. Numb.

Something in the wipers moving across the windshield formed a movie-flicker, but what he saw in the movie wasn't Father's face, it was Zoë's.

She smiled. It had been a long time since he'd felt her smile, how it could heat the room. And in these final moments he thought about how, sometimes, if he listened hard enough, he could hear the sounds inside her, how her sounds were his sounds, and that within her he could hear everything in the world breathing all at once.

Scarves of dirt lit by headlights.

Dirt in the cab, in his ears, mouth.

The concussion of his heartbeat and high keening of the engine.

Zoë's cat-green eyes, blinking up at him.

FIRST DAY's light hit the clouds capping the horizon, lighting them from beneath, orange and then violet in a sun she could not yet see. The knowledge that this was eastward useless to her. She turned around, watched the landscape color up and saw for the first time the distant bajadas leading to a mountain range, those blue cordilleras. Above them, white clouds looked paint-brushed across the sky in negative, like reflections in water, and she saw sea-foam in the cloud formations and thought, for a moment, that she was drowning, remembering Thurman telling her that the desert was once a seabed.

She told herself she was going above, back home.

Distant plant life afire. She expected to hear gulls screeching. Her synapses raged and burned, memories flaring through her mind; the jostle of the road; being hidden beneath the back-seat; senses overloaded by the terror of here, of the outside world, these desert flatlands.

She felt air warming her, heat-shimmering molecules.

Something moved through the creosote: slinking diamond-back, sidewinding, leaving scalloped tracks in its wake like puddled ice.

Home.

Then the sun came screaming across the land like a solar migraine.

She weaved an imaginary cat's cradle with her fingers, an old island custom to slow the sun's ascent, and she remembered with such clarity the argument she had with Ingrid the last time she saw her: the hot feel of the slap, and how she grabbed her satchel and left the cottage with Ingrid's words hissed behind her. Selfish little bitch. Wondering should she head for the hills of Asgard Fea because she couldn't bear another day with her head leaning against the classroom window. But she just sat on the harbor wall, waiting.

The silence of the sky was broken. She turned into the grey western light and heard a rhythmic thrum. She attempted to raise the shotgun to her shoulder but couldn't muster the strength. A chopper was coming low across the playa, dust storm raised by whirring blades, and in her mind a fog bank scrolled over her and the baked ground hit her in the face.

Heard blades thrumming.

Felt the chopper's engine throbbing, whirling dust into a frenzy.

Lying in the dirt, shielding her face from stinging particles.

She kept approaching the man whom no one noticed, the nobody who became her somebody. She didn't turn and run when she knew she should have. It was her fault. The struggle that wasn't a struggle, more like falling asleep and waking into nightmare, to the pulse of the engine, bound, gagged, in darkness alone. A noxious smell in her nose stinging her eyes and she kept vomiting into her mouth, having to swallow it, the cold maw of piss and scat between her thighs, caked behind her knees.

'No one can hear you scream. If you do, I'll cut the tongue from your head.'

He showed her the blade. She nodded. He removed the tape. Dreamy and drugged, 'I haven't handed in my home-work,' was what she said. These were the first words she ever said to him and he laughed.

She blinked. Saw the shadow of God's hand reaching across the sky.

'Can you hear me?' a man asked.

Can you hear me?

Americans and Canadians are united in their angry reaction today as details emerge of the escape and rescue of Zoë Nielsen who was kidnapped and held prisoner in a remote ranch house in Arizona for eight years. 'It's a disgrace that this can happen and for the authorities to know absolutely nothing about it,' said one caller to a Phoenix radio station as officers continued searching the ranch house of kidnapper Thurman Hayes. Unfortunately the girl's mother . . .

Phoenix's chief of police says Zoë is in a weakened state and is very ill, but alive, and is being treated at a secure location. He added that a Native American woman from a neighboring reservation alerted the sheriff to the situation but says the woman wishes to remain anonymous. He also refuses to comment on the kidnapper's whereabouts, only to state that Thurman Hayes is being held in police custody . . .

April 2008

Zoë returns to Arizona

FOREHEAD PRESSED against the scratched plastic of the window, she watches the city scroll below, and within each grid of intersecting roads, streets of white roofs create swirling patterns and the ridges of the high, sharp red mountains are like the veins on the back of a man's hand. Already she can make out blue rectangles and kidney-shaped swimming pools edged with Cyclone fences, city streets blanched by strips of desert scrubland and stamped with the black quadrangles of plazas and parking lots. In the distance, the foothills are defaced by implausibly green golf resorts below a sky that looks poisoned in the afternoon smog. The dusty mess of Phoenix, where women strut the noon-hot sidewalks almost naked and the obese roam like wildebeeste grazing on candy bars and cartons of fries. It has been almost a year since she was last here and today she is flying in under another assumed name on another fake passport.

She lowers the window blind, and then her eyelids.

They told her that she had been in a catatonic state for the first three days and that all she could do was lie in the hospital bed blinking. But she would remember so clearly the sound of her screams, babbling non-words towards the ceiling fan as the paper-smocked nurses, rubber soles squeaking, bowed before her as if in front of some kind of shrine, bringing their needles and swabs and expressionless looks. Her mind was so full of language it didn't make sense, pure phonetic sound filling her body like a fountain of blood. But the silence was a space where language could not go, a representation of pure pain, and she would remember watching the ceiling fans whirring round recalling the rotor-wash of the chopper's blades that saved her. She lay there thinking about the desert and the bloodied thing that came from her, like her insides had fused together and expelled the scar tissue of her former self. What brought her back into the present was hearing two cops talking in the corridor outside, about body dogs and aerial scanners. 'There may be others,' one of them said, and she felt the sudden, sickening heartspin of missing him.

The first words from her mouth: 'Where's Thurman?'

The room they moved her to had a wardrobe and cupboard and large bed. The wardrobe was full of clothes they had chosen for her and sat on top of the cupboard was a lamp, and beside the lamp an empty jewelry box the same color pink as her bed sheets. Above the cupboard hung a large oil painting of a yellow field of grass. At the edge of the field there was a farmhouse with a red-tiled roof and white walls, shaded by a large tree. It was summertime in the painting and stripes of afternoon sun fell through the clouds making the leaves on the tree glitter. Zoë would sit on her bed and stare at the painting, imagining she lived in that house with Thurman. A new start.

Someone she never got to see made her bed and tidied

up her things every morning; while she was in the interview room this unknown person was making her sheets
super-crisp and super-tight. She imagined it was Ingrid and
that the cops were keeping her hidden until she disclosed.
She loved sliding into the bed sheets at the end of the day,
lying pinned down while watching the TV that had certain
channels blocked, or reading the old newspapers and magazines, the air conditioner turned to its iciest blast above her.

Every night she had the same dream of Thurman standing
in the desert aflame. She would hear him crackling and the
smell of his skin was eerily just like bacon. He would hold
out a hand, heat melting the meat of his skull. 'Zoë?' And
every morning she would wake gasping, alarmed that she
was really there, in that unfamiliar room, away from him.

Her days were spent with the same two women, the
psychologist and the social worker, whose names she forgot
immediately. She was amazed by how they looked and talked,
acted and moved, the clothes they wore, the way they styled
their hair, their voices and skin and fingernails and eyelashes,
like they were another species. Then one day a strange
woman entered the interview room and Zoë recoiled.

'My name's Roberta, but my friends call me Bob.' She
pronounced it *Baaaaaab*. 'I'm a detective.'

Everything about Bob's face said laughter and sunshiny
days. She had perfect laser-white teeth behind wet, cushion-
lips, and buckeye-brown skin like nothing Zoë had ever seen
before. She wore a tight blouse and skirt that hugged her
figure just so, and her hair was sleek and straight as wind-
flattened grass. Zoë wanted to touch her, but instead she
scratched her scalp and then picked at her ears and nose
and examined her fingers with cross-eyes.

Bob said, 'Set yourself down, ladies.'

The detective, the psychologist, the social worker. Zoë's new coterie. Their severe, laid-back air and anodyne voices. Their effort-filled smiles.

What they saw was an eighteen-year-old girl who looked, and at times acted, more like a ten-year-old, and who, until today, had worn her silences like a glove, stunned by her unyielding mettle and will. But today was different.

Today they weren't showing her objects in plastic bags.

Today they hadn't brought those dumb, anatomically correct dolls.

Bob said, 'So tell me about Thurman.'

Lips open, unrealized words began falling from her mouth, eyes darting sideways as if she were being indiscreet. 'He's allergic to tumbleweed and the flowers of the bottle brush . . .' Such heat in her voice.

The women looked taken aback.

'He likes seeing cacti fattened by the rain and to see the Gila woodpeckers or elf owls nesting in them. He thinks it's wonderful how such beautiful birds can make a home in such ugly, spiky plants. I didn't know his name for eight years and I still don't know how old he is, but I know he's six feet tall and weighs 220 pounds and he has to have milk in his cup before the coffee is poured and he can't eat anything without salt. He knows the Latin name of every plant and animal and bird in the desert and he loved his mom more than life itself but says all women are whores. I can tell you how he was unsure of his memories and told himself lies just to make himself feel better. Can I get some food? Some fries and chocolate milkshake?'

Zoë stared at her socked feet while gestures were made,

and in the thud of silence came Thurman's last words: Don't you trust me? She asked, 'So you found him down in the bunker? He been arrested?'

No response.

'What's the date?'

'June 15, 2007. Today is a Friday.'

'So how long was I down there?'

'Eight years. Almost.'

'I mean in days, hours . . .'

In the fluttering of Bob's eyelids Zoë saw the on-off light of the bunker, the fade-in, fade-out. Bob turned to the psychologist and said, 'We'll get someone to work it out, if that's important to you?'

Zoë touched her scalp; her bald spot the size of an egg.

'What is it?' Bob asked.

They moved her here in the dead of night, talking to her like it was some kind of game, moving her to a room that smelled of latrine-cleaning products with a view of brick wall through a shaded window that wouldn't open and humorless male cops standing in the blue-carpeted corridor outside who would only let her leave to go down to the interview room with its table and mirrored wall and the camera in the top right-hand corner. Like being back in her tomb.

'You can't keep me prisoner. I ain't done nothing wrong.'

The things they asked about her life with Thurman, about the things they did or didn't do.

She closed her eyes, recalling her body warmth in the crisp bed sheets at night and missing the sight of Thurman's face in the morning, puffy-eyed, the lumpy sound of his morning-voice. The way she would pretend to stumble into him, to immerse herself within his strength.

'Tell me where they are . . . Ingrid? Thurman?'

Zoë the unwilling crime scene, the unyielding body of evidence; a living document refusing to disclose. The sheer volume of silence that had pervaded her life, it was manifest in the way she returned Bob's look.

The three women appeared to move closer, Bob always in front, treading towards her in slow motion as if they feared Zoë's personality would fracture. Their collective scrutiny was unnerving. Zoë squinched her eyes at the mirror on the wall and stuck out her tongue. The women shared looks; the psychologist nodded.

'Thurman is charged with false imprisonment, enslavement, coercion, rape.'

Unbidden she recalled the desert light in the gingery hairs along his arms as his hands moved to the back of her neck, the hot maw of his breath against her ear, *I love you.*

'I want to see him.'

'Do you understand, Zoë?'

'I want to go home. Back to the ranch. Coyote Plains.'

'You can't go back.'

'But I *need* to.'

The social worker looked at her askance.

'And why won't anyone tell me where Ingrid is? Nothing makes sense. I haven't done anything wrong and you're keeping me prisoner. You bitches are worse than Thurman ever was. Take your notepads and leave me alone. Get.' She stood up, pointing towards the door. 'I said get. Get the fuck out. And you people behind the mirror can go to fucking hell.'

But when the door was opened she said, 'Bob. I want Bob to stay.'

*

She tried to breathe normally, running her fingers across her scalp.

Bob forced a smile. 'Want me to do something with that?'

'What?'

'Your hair.'

Zoë bit her nails, shrugged.

'I was a beauty therapist in a past life. Worked in the biggest salon in the city. Had only been there a year when some punks held up the place.' She belly-laughed; it was so nice to hear. 'Whoever heard of robbers holding up a beauty salon? One held me hostage for over an hour with a pistol to my head. That's how I got into this business. Convinced him to give himself up. The cops said you ever thought of joining 'cos you a natural. So here I am. May I?'

Bob held out her hand; Zoë nodded.

Bob touched Zoë's hair, making a sound in her throat, and Zoë could smell Bob's perfume, thickly almond-scented. But she struggled not to bat Bob's hand away.

'I like you,' Zoë said, and Bob said, 'I like you too, hon.'

'You're not all namby-pamby around me.'

'You're a tough cookie. Maybe a little too tough.'

Zoë jerked her head away, narrowing her eyes. 'Why's that?'

Bob sat down and looked at Zoë tenderly. 'It's OK to cry, you know.'

'Never. Let him see the weakness in me and I'm dead. Why won't you let me see Ingrid?' What would Ingrid's voice sound like now? How would she look? 'Ain't *nobody's* fucking business,' she said, 'what went on there. So you better tell everyone that I'm *never* going to talk. Never going to break down and cry and say boo-hoo, Thurman did this

and did that. Get it? *Never*. Sooner I get home the better.'
She was beginning to get a sense of the gravity her eyes
could carry in a single glance. 'I want to see Ingrid. Want
to see her *now*.'

Bob shook her head slowly.

'There's something you need to know.'

It isn't the fanciest of hotels she could have stayed at, but it's close to the Medical Center, a place she's familiar with, and this makes her feel safer. She takes the Deluxe Suite, 500 square feet of chintz and clunky wooden furniture and two queen-sized beds covered with shiny patchwork quilts. In the courtyard outside an imposing marble fountain sits surrounded by palms, oleanders and Palo Verde trees. The purple wisteria around her window and the palm fronds beyond look like they have just been sprayed with water. Beaded. Glistening.

She opens the window and peers up: white crosshatches of airplane contrails are graved against the chrome-blue sky, and on the horizon there's the blush of the approaching sundown. Cicadas ring out from the Palo Verde trees but she can also hear another sound: below, a small birdcage hangs next to a doorway, a yellow canary hopping and singing inside the bars. She imagines it belongs to the beautiful Hispanic maid she saw in the corridor before.

She draws the curtains and sits on the bed and finds the NBC news channel and waits to see if there is any mention of her interview on Saturday. There is, and it makes her nervous.

She picks up the phone and orders beef burger with three large portions of French fries, extra crispy. Afterwards, she walks back over to the window and finds the canary has stopped singing but the cicadas are intensely loud and dumb moths tap out their Morse against the courtyard lights.

She found out later that they thought seeing Thurman would have shocked her into making that vital disclosure. They knew Thurman was never going to wake up; it was just a matter of days, hours; an infection had set in and was picking at his organs. Again her movements were made in the dead of night in unmarked cars beside plain-clothed officers, passing lighting rigs and TV cameras and trucks with satellite dishes, all wanting a glimpse of her, the girl who had spent eight years imprisoned underground, whom everyone had assumed was dead, but who made the amazing escape.

The hospital appeared empty. A state trooper, stationed outside a doorway, spoke briefly with Bob and Zoë heard him mutter something about a circus, about the Federal Building being under siege by the press, but Zoë heard 'the pressure' and felt her lungs tighten.

She was shown into a cramped room, greeted by a nurse with a sore-looking skin complaint that made Zoë feel dirty. The nurse passed her a pair of rubber gloves and a plastic apron. 'What do you understand of the situation?'

'You mean why the cops shot him?'

The nurse communicated silently with Bob.

'If only I hadn't run . . .' Zoë added, staring through the glass plate in the door where there was a sign on the wall saying: PLEASE LEAVE DOOR OPEN, AS BANGING IS DISTURBING PATIENTS. She thought this odd, considering.

'They told me that Thurman is in a coma, which means he is sleeping and might never wake up. I ain't dumb.'

Bob nodded once. The nurse folded her arms and said, 'Thurman has what we call a cranio-cerebral bullet wound. We had to operate to remove the bullet from his skull. The bullet's trajectory caused critical injuries to certain parts of his brain and he is sedated so that we can try to reduce the swelling around the damaged areas. Don't be alarmed by all the tubes going into him, they're keeping him alive.'

Zoë followed them into the room. She heard the sigh and bleep of machines and saw the shape of him in her eye-corner and began to pace the room like she was searching for him, calling for him quietly, 'Thurman? Thurman? *Thurman?* Thurman? *Thurman?*'

Bob's hand on her shoulder. 'Zoë.' Stern. Comforting.

Zoë stood perfectly still, mouth open, silent. It felt like a lifetime since she'd last seen him. His eyes were swollen, puffy. There were electrodes on the shaven areas of his scalp and fat tubes perforated his skull and throat and racks of machines bleeped and twinkled, crowding beside him.

Zoë began a nervous laugh, smelling her latex gloves as she covered her mouth.

'Is he dreaming?' Dreaming of a girl who never had to change, who would always be his perfect little princess.

'Maybe,' the nurse said. 'We can't really be sure.'

Zoë stepped towards him, prodding his thigh with a finger. Make him wake.

'It's OK,' Bob said. 'He can't hurt you no more.'

'Do you clean him? Bathe him, I mean?'

The nurse nodded. 'Yes.'

This stranger touching the mole on his left buttock, the scar on his inner thigh, the wispy halo of hair curling around his lower back.

Zoë watched the paper-smocked nurses and technicians attend to him. She observed the blood tests and syringe changes and brain graphing, keeping an eye on the machines measuring his heart rate, pulse, blood pressure.

He would have hated to be like this. He would have preferred to go out with a fight in the badlands of the desert, lying exposed on some rock, waiting for the buzzards or coyotes or lynx to come tear him apart.

The nurse lifted his eyelids and shone a light inside; Zoë imagined deep black space, like the reflection in an astronaut's visor. His body was there but Thurman was gone; he was an iceberg washed up on some foreign shore, thawing too slow for the eye to perceive, and once he had melted, she wondered, would there be an impression, a shadow? A dead seal lying on the beach?

The cage of his body. The tomb of his skull.

Bob crouched in front of her, blinking. It was time to leave. Zoë waved from the doorway. 'Goodbye, Thurman.' Staring at him, trying to fix the image of him in her mind.

The next morning they told her he had passed away during the night.

'His brain stem collapsed. I'm sorry.'

Suddenly there was another woman in the room. For a second Zoë thought it was Ingrid and she stepped towards her, opening her arms.

'Zoë, this is Anika.'

Anika smiled warily. 'Do you remember me, Zoë?'

'No. Where's Ingrid?'

The answer emerged on their faces.

A tragedy played out in their eyes.

'COULD YOU get some information for me?'

The greasy-looking receptionist blinks. 'Regarding what?'

'They's doing tours of Coyote Plains.'

'Oh.' The guy licks his uneven, goofy teeth.

Zoë notices these things, these tiny, physical imperfections in people. It's unsettling but she can't seem to stop doing it.

'The kidnapper's house?' he asks. 'Yeah. We had guests visit there just last week. Said they found it kinda creepy.'

Zoë clenches, unclenches her fists. 'Well, if you could just get me some prices and times I'd be real thankful.'

She shoulders her rucksack, puts on her pink-framed sunglasses and baseball cap and walks out into the Phoenix sun, burning away the morning clouds above. She walks across the scrubby lot to the KFC where she orders two meals, one of which she places in her rucksack. She sits at a red plastic table eyeing the distant bajadas, eating ravenously, even though she just polished off a full breakfast in the hotel restaurant an hour ago, her hunger an animal pacing the bars inside her. She finishes off the food, wiping her fingers on the legs of her bloom-pink tracksuit.

Two male cops cycle into the Drive-Thru and the fact they are wearing shorts amuses her. A yellow cab pulls in behind them; Zoë sees the driver is a woman.

She grabs the rucksack and heads for the door.

FALL 2007 and Zoë was back on the island, living with Red Bess at Dyna Point Lighthouse up on the shoulder of the cliffs, the tower a warning, white finger. It marked her return to the northern light, to its drama and intensity, to the eternal glut of Atlantic waves pulverizing the rocks 100 meters below, to the dirty, salty weather and horizontal rain. On clear nights the moonlight was agleam, shimmery twin reflected in the black plain of the sea, below nautical lights moving slow across the shelf of the world. Gulls hovered on updrafts outside, their cries like children in pain, the corded muscles of their wings and rude see-through eyes watching her through her bedroom window. Eastwardly window, next stop Norway, the land of her father.

Her bedroom was directly below the lantern gallery and used to be the old keeper's quarters. The room was bright and airy with a large double bed positioned in the center of the room with sailboat-patterned bed sheets and a quilted, seashell throw. There were aerial views of the sea and island through the high, arched windows, set into meter-thick walls. She loved sleeping in that room; she called it sleeping in the clouds. 'Up here in the sky,' she told Bess, 'it's the complete opposite of being down in my tomb.' Though as much as she loved that room she would feel a great shade of sadness and grief and loneliness lapping between its walls, trying to imagine herself back to the girl she once was, at home in the cottage with Ingrid a mere mile away. Eight years away.

The lighthouse had a tapered, octagonal shaft, reaching 30 meters high. Inside a spiral, steel stair connected the six floors. The four larger rooms beneath Zoë's held the kitchen, the bathroom, the living room, and Bess's bedroom – rooms that always smelled of rich, tangy food. The ground floor used to be Enchanted Lights, the candle shop where Ingrid worked, but was now used for storing boxes and logs and jerry cans of diesel for the impending winter months. There was herringbone, pitch-pine flooring throughout the light-house and nautical motifs above every lintel: sail boats, anchors, lanterns, seamen's compasses, seashells, crabs. There were wooden ship wheels on many of the walls and in the bathroom were mermaid towels and a lighthouse bath rug. On the living room wall, beside a ship's porthole clock, hung an enormous spear of a narwhal's tusk that gave Zoë the heebie-jeebies.

The high, narrow lighthouse, keeping her together in a way her past couldn't.

She had been home for two weeks, supposedly in secret, but still she found it hard to speak. There were sudden sulks and flares of anger; antsy retorts and strident, foul-mouthed questions. At times she remained stoical, tight-lipped, evasive; at others she became bossy and demanding. But there were also days when she couldn't get out of bed and days she wanted to die because her grief for Ingrid and

Thurman's absence was like somebody else living inside her skin, a second person with a second, stronger-beating heart, consuming her.

Thoughts about the baby they could have had.

Thoughts about the family they could have been.

If only the two of them had known, it might have changed everything.

And it was as if Bess sensed all of this. I'm trying my best not to pity you — these were the kind of looks Bess tried not to give but failed.

At night Zoë lay in bed listening to Bess roving the rooms below, to the sea-winds rotating the lighthouse walls with their high howl. This blustery other-world with its constant soundtrack of waves that took Ingrid's life. And she would hear things in the dead of night, thinking she was back in her tomb, like her brain had forgotten Thurman was in the ground 4,000 miles south. Her brain ever vigilant; it was exhausting. And nightly she imagined him burning in the desert, walking towards her in flames, his corpse leaning into her dreams.

In her bedroom she had a TV and a DVD player and an ever-growing stack of movies, novels and CDs. She spent comforting, indolent days submerged in the imaginary world of the books or the vacuum of cable TV and daytime soaps, languishing in her freedom. The movies made her restless and hungry for the world but she was a long way from being ready to leave the womb of the lighthouse. She would watch women on the screen amazed, but she felt like a bum loitering in a darkened doorway, too nervous to step out and join the complex, downbeat poetry of the world she saw distilled through the lens of a camera.

In the living room there was a PC connected to the Internet. Bess patiently taught her how to navigate sites, obviously surprised how quickly she picked things up. This was where Zoë saw the photo fit for the first time, the image some newspaper had created digitally of how they thought she might look now. The image looked nothing like her. She read all of the news articles and reports and bits of speculation about her time with Thurman and hated the lies she read. She found out that in her absence the world had changed, there had been earthquakes and tsunamis and floods and forest fires and terrorist bombings. Thurman was right: the world had turned to shit. And this is where she emailed or Google Chatted with Bob, three, four times a week. She got so excited when she saw the green dot next to Bob's name in the side panel, indicating Bob was online and available to chat.

Sometimes she went to one particular site that had a photograph of Thurman when he was a young man, his soph-omore year portrait. Zoë printed off the image and kept it hidden under her mattress along with her sneaky-pete stashes of candy. She would lie in bed and touch his pixellated face, a finger wet from her lips.

'Thurman.'

The linger of him.

THE DRIVER steers north along the palm-lined highway, the windshield striped by long morning shadows. She makes small talk, eating fries from the paper sack in her lap. 'Better watch my speed up here, yonder road's a favorite hiding spot for sheriff deputies looking to write their tickets. Yes, ma'am.'

'Sorry, but I'm not in the mood for chatting,' Zoë says.

'Fine by me. Mind some music?'

'Depends.'

The woman twists the dial on the stereo and eyes Zoë in the rear-view.

'This to your suiting?'

Zoë nods, watching how the city turns rapidly into suburbs, gated community after gated community of identical bungalows surrounded by mesquite and prickly pear. They pass trees with their trunks painted white to protect them from the sunlight and cross a bridge where a sign tells them there's a river below, but there is nothing down there but a wide expanse of dried-up bed, sparkling in the heat. They pass many roadside shrines, crosses covered in sunfaded, plastic flowers. Half an hour later the road runs into dirt and they are surrounded on either side by escarpments and cacti fields.

The woman shuts off the engine and turns to face Zoë.

'You sure you're gonna be OK, hon?'

'Pick me up from here in . . .' Zoë looks at her wrist where she wears both her grandfather's compass and a watch.

'This is a long way out of town.' The woman hooks a thumb over her shoulder. 'Gotta be careful in yon canyon. Rumored to be a mean-assed lion up there. They's getting desperate. Even drinking from folk's swimming pools. Attacked a man last month. Oh yeah. Tore him up *real* bad.' She looks Zoë up and down. 'You ain't exactly dressed . . .'

'At least you'll be able to find my body easy, once I've been mauled to death, that is.' Zoë points to a low over-hang to her right. 'You see that there, the shaded bit?'

'A-huh.'

'I don't plan going no further than that.' Zoë removes a hundred-dollar bill from her purse and hands it over. 'There'll be another one for you when you're back here at three. OK?'

'Yes, ma'am. You got plenty of water?'

Zoë nods. 'Don't call me ma'am.'

Zoë FELT like she shrank in the presence of adults, but Bess really was massive, a huge tree of a woman. She stood behind the kitchen table wearing a long flowery blue dress tied tightly in the middle with apron strings, a bowl sat in front of her. When the light hit her iron-gray hair at a certain angle you could still see the tinge of rust that she used to be famous for. Bess was moaning about her feet hurting and Zoë eyed her stout shoes, the dough balls of her ankles puffing over them.

Bess tipped the enormous bowl forward for Zoë to see. Chocolate. A bowl full of it. This was her way of coping: talking and cooking non-stop. Burgers with chunky, salty fries. Tapioca pudding. Jell-O. Treats of Oreos dipped in milk. Chocolate and candy and more chocolate. Fish — eight years without eating fish, and Zoë *adored* the tender white meat of snow crabs. All of this food Thurman never let her have.

Zoë had covered the mirror in her bedroom with a sheet, but it had nothing to do with her expanding waist size.

'The lighthouse was decommissioned last year, after they installed the radar system down in the harbor. The walls are completely solid,' Bess said, as if Zoë were afraid the place might collapse. 'Ashlar quoins and interlocking granite coated with Puzzellani, volcanic material from Mount Etna, a volcano in —'

'Sicily. I ain't dumb.'

'Sorry. I forgot you're a walking encyclopedia.'

'You haven't changed, you know.'

'I wouldn't call the menopause and early retirement no change, or the fact I'm growing a beard and turning deaf.'

Zoë laughed, eyeing the small, flesh-colored hearing aids in Bess's ears that she called 'Mork and Mindy'.

'But the beard suits you,' Zoë said.

'That *voice*.'

'What?'

'The Devil speaks with an American accent.'

Zoë remained silent, averting her gaze, scared Bess would see that second person staring out of her eyes, giving her away.

'Make yourself useful,' Bess said. 'Grease this tin for me.' Bess ripped a piece of paper from a block of butter and showed her what to do.

Zoë asked, 'Why you never married?'

Bess snorted a laugh. 'Impudent and fond, you are.'

'You never fancied having kids?'

Zoë watched Bess begin to move and strain, hypnotized by the wrinkled pink skin swinging from her arms. As she mixed she hummed a little tune. She looked at Zoë and smiled her many-chinned smile. Zoë looked away. Above them a long creel railway-tracked across the ceiling with stripy blue tea-towels hanging down. Over against the far wall an Aga stood, huge hulk of black metal.

'We can go out whenever you want, you know. I've got some old clothes and wigs and stuff we used for the Christmas play last year. We could make you a disguise. It might be fun.'

'I'm happy here.'

'You need some air, some sunlight. You're whiter than a fish's belly.'

'Good.'

Later, when they ate at the table together, Zoë kept seeing Thurman falling to his food and heard those horrible noises he made. His wobbly nose.

Her skin still wanted his skin. Her eyes still craved his eyes, her fingers his fingers. She wanted to exchange breaths through open lips. Wanted to feel him watching her from above like a hunter. The rawness of her body afterwards; the physical rawness of his absence from her world.

'The way you stare, it unnerves me,' Bess said.

'Sorry. I'm just getting used to it, that's all.'

'Used to what?'

'Living with someone else. Seeing someone else's face every day.'

'You're adjusting.'

'What was I like before I disappeared?'

Bess's expression was composed of equal parts nostalgia and sorrow. 'You were very independent. You'd go beach-combing alone, wandering along the Sound and cliff-edges. You enjoyed your own company. And you always spoke to adults like you were an adult, because Ingrid always treated you that way.'

She found it hard to imagine.

*

Bess measured Zoë for her first bra and failed to hide her pain when she saw the ribbons of scars across her breasts and nipples. Bess hugged her tightly, silently, preferring to do her weeping in private.

She bought Zoë stacks of drawing materials and quickly the walls of the lighthouse began to fill with torn-out pages, illustrations of the view from her bedroom windows, the one pointing eastwards towards the Atlantic, the other westwards, towards Gulber Voe and the hills of Asgard Fea. This need to draw, it was the only thing that had remained constant in her life, and Zoë seeped into the silence of every blank page. That is why she needed to draw the landscapes around her, to fix herself in time and place.

Some nights she would climb into Bess's enormous bed and lie there, perfectly still, listening to Bess sleep-breathing.

Some nights she would stand on the threshold inhaling the night air, sensing the circle of the island and the circle of the lighthouse mirroring the wheel of thoughts in her head, too scared to leave the safety of the lighthouse walls, because even in his absence, even with all this distance, even though she knew that he was gone, she could feel his looming presence, his threat stalking the corridors inside her, sniffing between her legs, nostrils flaring like a dog's at the very core of her world.

The quality of silence by the sea was different to that of the desert. Beside the sea silence wasn't an absence of sound, it had a density and climate, wind stirring and containing it, folding and tucking. Beyond the ceaseless rhythm of the breakers below, and the pulsebeats of her own heart, she noticed this thick wall of silence. She hid in there sometimes.

One night Bess rolled over and asked, 'Who were you talking to?'

Zoë climbed out of bed. 'Myself. Leave me alone.'

'You're crying. Let me draw you a hot bath.'

'Screw you,' she snapped.

'Don't be throwing a conniption fit on me, young lady.'

With her hand on the doorknob, Zoë looked over her shoulder. 'Sorry.'

'Come back to bed, sweety.'

Zoë didn't budge. She felt dislocated in time and space.

'You're never alone, you know that. I'm always here.'

'I know I'm never alone, that's the problem.'

Zoë's favorite movie was *Thelma and Louise*. She liked to pretend she was Geena Davis as Thelma, and Bob was Susan Sarandon as Louise. She knew most of the script by heart and would sound-bite the dialogue. It would whisper through her dreams.

'Talk nice to her when she calls, women love that shit.'

The men in the movie, they reminded her of Thurman in his wife-beater, sweating on the veranda, so consistently irritable that it became normalized and she found it funny. She found it cute and knew that was wrong.

Zoë would applaud when Thelma almost gets raped but Louise shoots the guy dead. She had faith in these movie stars because they made the implausible plausible; they became somebody else.

She wanted to be a fugitive on the road, Thurman driving them away in a 1966 Thunderbird convertible heading for Mexico, being pursued along dusty highways by Harvey Keitel across a landscape she recognized as home. She wanted to have a wild night in a dirty motel room, learning what all the fuss is about.

'Whenever Zoë has fun with men, something terrible happens.'

Even after all the credits had rolled, that final scene made her sob for a long time, the stark beauty of it. It had been a long time since she'd cried like that; a long time since the early days of the bunker when the act of crying was too physically painful because the places those tears came from had turned to stone, when all her screaming had parched her throat and clogged her sinuses. Often she would wonder about that night Thurman drove her out to a canyon some-place, blindfolded, with her hands tied behind her back. He made her walk for a long time and when they stopped he stood in front of her, undid her blindfold and asked her to tell him how much she loved him. 'Before I kill you.'

'Do it,' she whispered.

His girlish screams echoed off the canyon walls like the sound of hell, and when the echoes stopped she asked, 'What do you want from me?'

Dark silence.

'Everything.'

THE BODY beneath the tracksuit, heavy bones and rolling flesh, legs and lungs aching and sweat pooling in the hollow where the collarbones meet and dip. She scans the ground for anywhere a rattler or scorpion or tarantula may hide, but the nook has been carved by centuries of wind, smooth as porcelain. She sits in its shade, rucksack between her legs, and removes her sunglasses. Blinking, she scans the plain of the city below, stretching between the distant clinch of mountainsides. Out there, to the south-west, just beyond the horizon, lays the table-flat desert surrounding Coyote Plains. She sucks the drink from her bottle and then shoves some cold clammy fries in her mouth.

Other people touching her things down in her tomb.

She leans her head back against the rock, watching dust devils roil between mute and naked trees. She licks her lips, mouth so dry in this heat, and she can still taste the maple syrup she had on her waffles at breakfast this morning.

She thinks about Thurman's brain wiped smooth as a pebble, a hole through its centre like the one she wears on a string around her neck.

She places the pebble in her mouth and sucks.

Ranger Anika called at the lighthouse regularly. From the moment they sat beside each other on the flight back from Phoenix, Zoë had warmed towards this mousy, nervous woman. It was Zoë's first time on an airplane and Anika sat beside her in silence. Zoë watched the clouds as they nudged dreamily through the ozone, thinking she wanted to stay up there forever.

There were the sporadic health checks by the local doctor, who seemed amazed she wasn't falling sick all the time. 'Your immune system ain't used to other people,' he said. But Zoë refused to speak to the island's psychiatrist, the same grave-looking man that Ingrid had refused to speak to.

Zoë asked again, 'You haven't told anyone I'm here?'

'No. But they're not stupid,' Anika said.

'I feel like that monster,' Bess said, and Zoë said, 'Please don't.'

'It's horrible, keeping her locked up here, scared anyone might see. I know why we're doing it, but the whole affair makes me feel so uneasy. Besides, everyone knows.'

Zoë asked, 'Really?'

There were the occasional knocks at the front door, of photographers and journalists and nosy islanders. One day Zoë saw a man with a long-lensed camera hiding in the laurel bushes down the cliff path; Bess chased him away with her walking stick. But most of the press, Bess told her, didn't even make it as far as the harbor. The islanders had become wary of strangers. Even the hotels were showing allegiance.

'Folk keep nodding at me, winking,' Bess said. 'Especially the shop owners and the postman, delivering all these movies and what not. But it's one good thing about this place, a misguided sense of loyalty. They'll protect you, the whole island. I think they feel guilty.'

Anika shot Bess a look, staring through the holes in Bess's tact.

Zoë asked, 'What about?'

'Ingrid. They treated her *so* bad when you went missing.'

Zoë walked to the window where wind-blown raindrops sashayed in runnels down the pane.

'They said Ingrid had given you away. Sold you to Gypsies who would sell your organs. Or gave you up for illegal adoption.'

'That's so dumb,' she said, her breath fogging the glass.

'It's just human nature. People waving their fingers at things they don't understand. Was too much for people to comprehend. But you're here now and everything has changed. You've brought hope back to the island. Hope.'

Anika said, 'My friend, she's got a daughter your age. Says you were at school together . . .'

'I don't want to meet her.'

'I didn't mean that. I've just been asking what girls your age are into, clothes and make-up and music and all that. So I brought you some stuff.'

Anika passed her a heavy bag. 'Welcome home, sweety.'

'Let me clean. Please. I *need* to.'

'But *he* made you do that, didn't he?'

'Look, I just got to do it. Please.'

'You don't got to, it's my house.'

'Gee, thanks.'

'I mean it's your home, Zoë. But I want to look after *you*.'

They had been arguing for quite some time when Zoë snatched the yellow duster from Bess's hand and Bess sighed the sigh of the beaten woman.

So Zoë blitzed the rooms of the lighthouse as often as she felt the need. 'Place never looked so clean,' Bess would say half-heartedly, obviously worried Zoë was approaching some kind of meltdown. 'But don't you think you should give it a rest?' It was just another adjunct to her worries and guilt.

It was during one of these manic cleaning sessions that Zoë found the letter. She wasn't snooping or looking for anything in particular, she was just absentmindedly dusting and riffling through Bess's things while Bess was at the shops and she found a small square of folded paper.

The handwriting was so similar to Zoë's it made her head spin.

I am sorry to do it like this, but I have to leave, and I hope you won't hate me for what I am about to tell you. I came here wanting to help, but it seems to me you have already given up. I don't see the point in me being here any more. I have tried to tell you but there never seemed a right time. I have another child with a woman in Oslo, a little boy. His mother won't let me see him and her father has threatened me. But I am going back now to try and make things right. And you will probably find out from the Rangers that I came back here four years ago but I didn't leave the ship. If

I'd known about Zoë I would have returned. I would. But you kept her from me and I will never understand that. I just thought you needed to know. You told me your mother warned you that I was a useless bastard but please don't think that about Zoë's father. You hurt me when you told me that because you laughed. I have no right to ask you to forgive me but this is what I wish. I will keep looking for our daughter. I will do everything I can. I just can't be here any longer. It is too painful. I am leaving for us both.

 Jon

That night, Bess sat knitting in her rocking chair, telling Zoë stories about her grandparents. Zoë watched the flames inside the pot-bellied stove move warm colors across Bess's wrinkled face, the rhythmic clicking of her needles like some desert insect calling for a mate in the dead of night, hungry for Bess's memories. More, more.

'As Ingrid lay there, swollen, in total agony, with eclampsia I think it was, your grandmother clucked and cooed, rocking you in her arms as she paced the cottage, singing nursery rhymes in the old way. Ingrid never left the crib's side, scared you might be stolen away, or worse: you'd change in some way, become a fairy child. A changeling.'

'My grandmother was a witch, wasn't she?'

Bess stopped knitting. 'You're a lot like her, you know'

'And my father always knew about me, didn't he.'

It wasn't a question.

SHORTLY AFTER her setting up an email account, Bob sent her a message apologizing for bringing bad news. There were three unsolved cases they were trying to link to Thurman, one involving a fifteen-year-old girl who disappeared from her uncle's motel twenty miles east of Coyote Plains, back in 1999. Her uncle just figured her for a runaway but when he saw Thurman's photograph on TV he recognized him. The FBI were involved.

I'm sorry, Zoë, she wrote. But Thurman did some really bad things. I thought I better tell you before you see it online or in the press.

But all Zoë could think about was why Thurman hadn't killed her too.

He must have loved her. He must have.

Winter dragged. The long dark nights and short gray days seemed to go on forever and the tempest and gloom left her feeling low and she craved the Arizona sunshine. She peered between snaggletooth icicles and snow crystals on her windowpane, out across the plain of ice-spotted sea, blinking silently, feeling shipwrecked by the anger she felt, caused by their complete absence from her world. Ingrid's. Thurman's.

She waited, picturing Bob sat in a darkened room 4,000 miles south, her face lit by the blue light of the computer screen, biting her nails, wondering how best to respond.

> Bob is typing . . .
> **Bob**: it was evidence. The baby would have been photographed and DNA obtained by an independent medical team and then, I'm sad to say, destroyed. I'm sorry.
> **me**: thank you.
> **Bob**: you understand we had to be careful about what we told you.
> **me**: thank you for your honesty. Got to go.
> **Bob**: wait. Your father has been in touch with us again. He says he's heard you're back on the island and is threatening to visit. Are you sure I can't give him your email address?
> **me**: yep I'm sure, I'm not ready to talk with him. Speak later x

She stared at the screen a long time.

> Bob is offline. Messages you send will be delivered when Bob comes online.

Zoë noticed her clothes were getting tight and more than one pair of pants were impossible to button. She decided that from now on all she would wear were tracksuits like the ones she'd seen people wearing on the bus-fumed streets of Phoenix. She ordered seven pairs off the Internet with Bess's card, one for each day of the week, Adidas Original Firebird Women's Track Suits with three stripes down the arms and legs. She ordered them in teal, solid blue, collegiate aqua, black, bloom-pink, purple, and celadon-gray, all in XL. When the packages arrived she was delighted to find they had given her a complimentary baseball cap with her order, bloom-pink, which she wore everywhere, even while watching TV in bed.

Bob: so many letters and prayers.
me: that's nice. I suppose they think God rescued me?
Bob: you've even got letters from men asking to marry you.

Zoë read the words in disbelief.

Bob is typing . . .
Bob: you there?
me: even when I was down there and I knew I was down there for good and never getting out, I knew that he was above, thinking the same thoughts as me, like we was dreaming and thinking the same things. Me wanting him to come down and him wanting to come down. To make things right between us, that's all we wanted.
Bob: i don't know what to say.

Zoë found the cardboard box beside her bed one morning, thinking it was more disguises for the nightly drives around the island in Bess's Oldsmobile.

She pulled the objects out onto the floor and spread them about her:

a book, *The Magic Faraway Tree* by Enid Blyton;
a wrist compass;
two cassette tapes, one labeled 'Zoë's Songs', the other 'Ingrid's Songs';
a pink blanket;
a heavy wool pajama unit suit;
a stuffed toy rabbit.

She touched each object in turn, attempting to divine their history through her fingertips. She couldn't remember the book or what the story was about though the foisty smell of the pages reminded her of a teenage girl. It made no sense.

She must have worn the unit suit when she was an infant, but it may as well have belonged to another child. She held the suit to her face and inhaled; the only image she received seemed unconnected, of being sat beneath a Christmas tree, staring up through branches and fairy lights.

She held the stuffed rabbit to her chest, inhaling its dusty smell, and knew she had slept with it every night, the two of them lying in the bedroom dark, listening to music coming from the living room, looking over towards the door where there was a safe crack of light, a warm orange glow coming from the hallway. The sounds of Ingrid out there.

Zoë walked downstairs and slid the cassette labeled 'Ingrid's Songs' into the machine and pressed 'play'. The sound of an electric piano filled the room, notes like bubbles and a woman's voice, high and desolate. Behind Zoë came the sound of Bess singing along, not quite making the high notes.

Eyes closed, face smeared with a smile, Bess stood there swaying while the singer's voice soared, gutsy and soulful, feathery like birdsong. But there was no memory of this song. Nothing. When the song finished she turned down the volume and waited for Bess to speak. Bess appeared shaken.

'Joni Mitchell. You must have heard this song a thousand times. My God, you really don't remember?'

'My memories only come back as dreams, but when I wake up . . .'

Embers pinged against the inside of the pot-bellied stove.

Bess sat in her rocking chair and fell to her knitting, as if the past few minutes hadn't occurred.

'But I remember this girl,' Zoë said. 'Upstairs, I mean, when I saw the children's book. I remembers a girl reading to me, but she was wearing sunglasses?'

Bess laughed like a drain.

'I'm not imagining things?'

'No,' Bess said. 'She was the priest's daughter. Used to baby-sit for you sometimes. The girl was completely blind.'

'I had a *blind* babysitter?'

'Sure did.'

They both laughed.

Zoë rubbed her stomach contemplatively, affectionately. The joy of recollection. 'But I remember her *reading* to me.'

'Well, she probably had a good imagination.' Bess clicked her fingers. 'Elizabeth. She left for the mainland years ago. A gifted musician she were. Cellist.'

Zoë felt a comedown; she wanted to meet this girl again.

'You must remember Elizabeth's mother? Crazy? This woman wrote the rulebook. They had one of these rare-breed huskies, a big, walking fur ball. Samoyed. Well, she used to brush this dog every day and collect the wool and knit sweaters from it. She made poor Elizabeth wear them to school. Good job the girl was blind, they were awful.'

'I *hate* dogs,' Zoë said. She went over to the stereo and replaced the cassette with 'Zoë's Songs', but when she pressed 'play' it spooled and the machine ate it. She stared at it, saying nothing.

That night Bess sat on the bed beside her, brushing her hair. A nightly routine that made Zoë uncomfortable but she knew it made Bess happy.

'Your bald spot has completely gone,' Bess said. 'You can't even see the stitches no more.'

'Will you read to me?'

Bess gazed down at her with lead-blue eyes. Fishy, storm-filled.

Zoë passed her the book and Bess read the story about Jo, Bessie and Fanny, the Saucepan Man and Dame Washalot and Moonface and Silky. Zoë loved the idea of the Land of Birthdays but not the Land of Take-What-You-Want. Zoë listened intently to the music of Bess's voice, the leisurely, drifting lilt, her sentences lifting and then smashing at the apex like waves, and it saddened her that she no longer spoke like that. Once Bess finished reading Zoë said, '*We* live in the Faraway Tree. Here, the light-house in the clouds.'

Bess pushed hair behind Zoë's ear. 'I see Ingrid in you so clearly, you know. You two are so alike, in spirit.'

Zoë rolled over in bed, burying her face into Moppy's fur.

Bess asked, 'Why do you never talk about her?'

'I said I'd come tomorrow, didn't I?'

She put on the long black wig and fleece hat and they left the lighthouse, an eerie light spreading across the line of horizon like blueberry jam. Above them the feathery wisps of the Aurora hung, and watching them swirl she recalled the green lights of the machine scanning Thurman's heart rate.

They took the path above the town, her homecoming path, and with each step she was walking back in time, eight years too late. The lost lanes of childhood. Zoë checked her grandfather's wrist compass as if it might tell her something and in the dark distance came the sound of a dog barking. The scars on her legs began to tingle.

'Come on,' Bess took her arm, 'it's OK.'

The woebegone cottage with its boarded-up windows and flaking paint and roof tiles missing, sagging cottage knit tightly with black slate. Bits of string and knots were hung around the doorway; the doorway Zoë left that morning back in 1999 with Ingrid stood on the threshold screaming down the lane at her.

Bess took the key from her pocket and stepped towards the door.

'No,' Zoë said. 'Don't.'

Bess whipped her head in Zoë's direction. 'But you remember the place, don't you?'

Zoë kicked at the ground, shrugged her shoulders. 'I've been pretending to remember a lot of things because it upsets me too much to admit I don't. But when I saw you, I knew your face and voice. Really. Truly.'

Bess folded her arms, obviously too sad for words.

Zoë asked, 'Why is no one living here?'

'They couldn't sell it. I tried to keep an eye on it, but over the years things happen. Technically it's yours, you know. We could start to make plans to do the place up.'

Zoë shook her head. 'No. What's with all the knots?'

'The islanders think it's infested. Evil spirits.'

Zoë sneered through a laugh. 'That fisherman Ingrid knew?'

Bess smiled, nodded. 'Einar?'

'I dreamt of him a lot.'

'He was accused of taking you. Had to leave the island.'

'No.'

'The Rangers had to blame someone. The folk here . . .'

Zoë bit her lips.

'Ingrid decorated your bedroom, just before . . . you know. She always left your bedroom light on at night and your curtains open. Just in case. She told me she used to go in there and pretend to rock you to sleep because she thought she could hear you crying . . .'

Rain fell grayly across the quiet island.

'Maybe she could?'

Bess pretended not to hear. 'It's your nineteenth birthday next month. Have you thought about the future? You need a dream to help pull you through.'

Zoë pointed down the glebe towards the Sound. Teeth chattering with cold, she said, 'I want to see her.'

The spring moon was high, and a blue, wet light was spreading upwards from the east, illuminating skifts of snow drifted against drystone walls. Waves, out of sight, died against the beach with breathy sighs, and across the Sound the black mass of Klibo rose to an awesome height. Zoë walked down the glebe, remembering how she'd dreamed about Ingrid searching for her up in those hills and moorland bluffs, calling her name. A name that no longer felt like hers.

They walked between the ragged teeth of tombstones, epitaphs flickering before her eyes. Her tracksuit bottoms, dew-wet from the grass, formed a deliciously cold halo about her ankles. A sudden swap of wind seized her mind, flipping it in a new direction, wondering if any of Thurman's family was buried here.

Bess leaned down with a crack of her knees and started fussing around the headstone, lifting dead flowers wrapped in cellophane.

'I tries my best to keep it tidy, but this damned grass.'

Zoë imagined the mason carving her mom's name, blowing dust from the letters. *Ingrid Nielsen.* Remembering the marble crosses beneath the Palo Verde tree.

Marny. Dear Mom.

Sea birds began testing the dawn air; their calls felt so crude.

Bess stood up and pointed. 'Your grandmother's over there. Near yon tree.'

At the far end of the cemetery a pathetic tree stood bent by decades of sea winds, rimed branches etched against the brightening sky. Beyond the wall, fawn-colored sand dunes bent and rolled, clouds hanging heavy like the ache in her head.

A few human-shaped, bobbing seal heads watched her from

the waves. She pictured Ingrid on the beach, walking into the cold mouth of the water. She waved towards the seals and asked, 'What was the last thing Ingrid ever said to you?'

Bess's expression darkened.

'Please. Just say it.'

Bess looked back up the glebe towards the cottage, and after a moment she said, '"I can't face a lifetime without finding her, a lifetime of trying not to forget Zoë. But all I'm left with is myself, and . . ."' Bess paused, letting the words take shape.

'And what?'

Bess's voice was iceberg-cold, '"And myself isn't such a nice place to be."'

Zoë told herself not to react. Beside her feet she noticed a small, sea-polished pebble that had a hole through one end. She picked it up and stroked the sand from its surface, wondering where it had come from. And suddenly, vivid as her own hands, she remembered a summer day many years before, lying on a blanket on the sun-worn beach beside Ingrid, the scent of coconut oil on Ingrid's skin and the lemon juice in her hair that she said helped bleach it blonder. They were lying side by side, touching hands, smiling up into the sunshine while Ingrid sang a melody to herself, the melody on the 'Ingrid' tape, Joni Mitchell's 'Woodstock'. Zoë even remembered the walk back home for supper, her swimming costume sea-damp and cold beneath her clothes, her skin sorely pink along the strap lines, rubbing against her woolen sweater. Those summer evenings when it never seemed to darken fully, when it felt like they were the only two people living on the island, when they moved around each other in silence because they knew what it was like to live in each other's skin.

'Do you still have any of Ingrid's candles that she made?'
Blinking, Bess cleared her throat, nodded.

'And Einar,' Zoë said. 'That fisherman, Ingrid's boyfriend.
I want the Rangers to find him. Can we do that?'

Bess wiped her eyes. 'This wind,' she said.

That afternoon Zoë climbed up into the lantern gallery and
arranged the candles along the windowsill. The 360-degree
views revealed wind-driven snowflakes large as her palm.
She was in a snow cloud. Her eyes lost focus and she could
read the patterns in the snow like the rills of a fast-flowing
river. It was mesmerizing, the snow blown by horizontal
winds that Bess called *screevars*.

She considered the lantern, its optic giving out six flashes
every thirty seconds. Bess told Zoë the beam could travel
twelve miles out to sea, the distance of all sea horizons, and
Zoë thought about all the sailors' and fishermen's lives it
must have saved.

In the louring light she lit Ingrid's candles and sat on
the gallery floor, hugging her legs, rocking in the yellow
flicker.

It was her message to the waves: I ain't angry with you
no more.

She typed her name into the search engine. One item was
about Jon.

Exclusive interview with father of kidnapped girl . . .

She was about to open it when she saw the link to
YouTube.

Video of Zoë Nielsen dungeon.
This video was filmed by the Tohono Mining Company.

She clicked 'play'.
There was an external shot of the garage door. Someone opened the door from inside and then quickly stepped away so they couldn't be seen. There was an orange-colored rectangle on the garage floor with the number 16 printed on it.
Coyote Plains.
The cold distance she felt between here and there, then and now, moved inside of her like Thurman's fingers. She felt utterly violated.
It was that night that she had her first dream about Ingrid drowning. She saw the ellipses of bubbles rising from Ingrid's mouth, blinking up at the morning light spangling on the sea's surface, a skitter of capelin flashing before her face, metallic scales like passing memories. Panicking, flailing against the water, against herself, she paused, falling into the sea's gloaming world. Something, someone, had been waiting for her. Someone was dragging her down.
'Ingrid?'
It was me, Zoë thought.
It was all my fault.

She asked Bob how the video could ever have been allowed. In the responding email Bob explained what had happened to Coyote Plains. The place had undergone a full forensic investigation that ended a few weeks after Thurman died and when everything was completed the court handed the keys back to its rightful owners, the Tohono Mining Company, who had bought the land from Thurman just before Zoë escaped.

So he was planning to leave. Planning a future that didn't include her.

She wondered about her birthday meal, whether it was some kind of farewell. How close had she been to death? She would never know.

Bob said they were trying to find evidence to corroborate the fact that both she and Thurman were actually there, and that the ranch would have been left exactly as it was the night she escaped. Any information she disclosed would have to have been verified forensically, even though she told them little. A whole host of people such as furniture makers and electricians would have taken the place apart and then reassembled it like they had never even been there. Analysts and researchers began looking into past and unsolved crimes in the area; specialized choppers took aerial photos of the property and body dogs would have been out there sniffing for human remains.

Bob also wrote that the state police had their own journalists in the media and that while Zoë was in Phoenix there had been daily briefings with press officers and continual risk assessments of the media's influence and they had even had to appoint a media lawyer to deal with all the requests for interviews that were flooding the desk.

There had been over 500.

I know you hate the telephone and you told me not to call, but please, if you need to talk, you know I'm here. I'll always be here for you, Zoë. You know that, don't you?

Zoë's response was:

> I want you to do one thing for me. Find out how much
> the mining company paid for Coyote Plains and I'll do
> an interview. Exclusive. One-off. But I want to be paid
> exactly the same amount they paid Thurman for the
> ranch. No more, no less. It's what I'm owed. Then I'll
> come back to Arizona and do it. But my identity must
> be protected. I don't want my face to be shown and
> I'd like you to come with me.
>
> Plus I've got to get off this goddamn island. It's driving
> me nuts.
>
> And I want to take you up on your offer. I want to
> change my name and identity, like witness protection,
> whatever. You know I said it feels wrong because I can't
> get Ingrid's approval and all. She was my mother, you
> know. But I need to. Not this silly fake passport stuff
> but the whole works, like you said I could. I'm sick of
> being a stranger to myself. I need to become someone
> else.
>
> For good.

Far down on the ladder of sleep, she saw Ingrid beneath
the waves again, her mother's lips a perfect O, expelling
the punctuation of life. Water whirled into her and the sea
began to boil. Moving sideways across her eyes, like two
curtains, Ingrid's life was extinguished, but still a dim spark
flickered. Asleep, Zoë reached out her hands into the

bedroom dark and they threaded fingers together, mother and daughter touching in this liquid heaven, the tidal surge making their bodies sway, mother and daughter dancing, two shape-shifting shadows, down below where dreams are made, where other lives are lived.

She took all her drawings from the lighthouse walls and tore them into tiny pieces, dropping them from her window to the waves below, watching them fall like snowflakes, making her smile. Then she removed the sheet from the mirror in her bedroom and spoke to her unfamiliar reflection.

'You can do this,' she said.

You can.

BOB IS waiting to greet her in the doorway of Tee Pee Mexican Diner. They embrace quickly, tightly.

Bob holds her at arm's length. 'You look different.'

'You mean fat. You weren't followed, were you?'

Bob sucks her teeth. 'Should we eat?'

'Yeah, I'm wasting away.'

The host shows them to a booth at the back and because the place is quiet the waitress is here immediately, poised to scribble in her palm pad. Zoë points to what she wants and Bob orders for her. Once the waitress is gone, Zoë says, 'I went walking in the hills before. It's been the first time, properly, out on my own. No one waiting for me, watching me.'

'What you get up to out there?'

She shrugs. 'I'm still scared of anyone touching me. Scared of them accidentally brushing against me. How I'll react. I keep wishing I were invisible.'

Bob looks away for a moment.

'I know what you're thinking,' Zoë says. 'You should hear Bess going on at me, her of all people. But this is healthy fat compared to before, not being starved-to-death half the time. It does something to you, being so close to death so often.' Remembering those foregone days, battling self-pity. 'This is dignified fat,' she says.

Bob clears her throat. 'The interview . . .'

'My medicine.'

Bob puckers her forehead. 'The papers are all signed with NBC, and you got the full protection of the squad behind you. One camera, one interviewer, one hour, as you specified. And I'll be there with you. We'll use the secure unit you stayed at when you left the hospital, if that's OK?'

The oil painting on the wall, the farmhouse surrounded by long yellow grass, her and Thurman living there in peace.

'Yeah.'

'It won't be weird for you, being back there?'

'Weird is my middle name.'

The waitress arrives with drinks on a tray and rearranges the silverware. When the waitress is gone Bob asks, 'So what you gonna say?'

Zoë drinks her juice through the straw and then wipes her mouth with the napkin. 'I'm gonna tell the whole world to go mind their goddamn fucking business.'

Bob frowns. An evaluating gaze.

Zoë asks, 'Has Jon been in touch again?'

'Yeah.'

'Blood or not, I just ain't ready.'

'Well, that's your prerogative. What's that on your wrist?'

'My grandfather's compass. He used it at sea. Direction is more important than time. Bess told me that.'

Bob's laser-white smile.

'I know I joke around and stuff, in my emails, moaning about her 'n'all. But I know I'm lucky. Bess gets me, you

know. She ain't pushy. And she's direct. No messing
around.'

'It's important you have a woman in your life. Positive
female figure.'

'Other than you?'

Bob beams.

'I wish me and Ingrid could choose a name together, you
know. Does that sound dumb?'

'No.'

'But I get to choose it, if that's all right?'

'Course.'

'I don't want nothing goofy.'

Bob nods.

'Or a man's name.'

They laugh. Their meals arrive and Zoë falls to her plate
like a woman starved. Eating in silence, exchanging glances.

When Zoë finishes she says, 'You know how some people,
when they mess up or are in a lot of trouble, they fake their
own deaths to disappear? I guess I'm doing the opposite.
Have a fake life to escape, to survive. I kinda like the name
Geena, as in Geena Davis.'

Bob's eyes sparkle. She gives Zoë a twisty smile. 'So you've
been thinking about the future?'

'I want to go to college. Study.'

'Let me guess.'

Zoë nods, wiping her mouth on the napkin and scrunching
it into a ball. 'I want to come back to the States. It's my
home. I want to study in a city full of people and noise
every second of every day where no one will know who I
am and no one will give a damn. I want to live in an apartment with lots of windows and lots of light, learning

269

how to draw and paint for real. I want to learn about color.'
Her eyes seek approval.

Bob laughs gently.

'I want to be an anonymous nobody. To be fat and wear
workout clothes. I want to live somewhere with no seasons
other than hot, miles from any sea or beach. I want to spend
a night with a man like Brad Pitt and understand what all
the fuss is about.'

Bob laughs harder. 'It's so nice to see you, I can't tell
you. We ain't meant to get attached. In the job, I mean.'

'If Thurman knew I'd be friends with a cop . . .'

Bob pretends not to react, but does, and Zoë gives her
a drifty look because she is gazing in at the images in her
head, eyes staring inward.

'The money,' Zoë says. 'I'm giving Bess some of it so she
can retire in style. Go on a cruise for a few years. I owe
her. She put her heart around me, unconditional, you know.
And I know the interview will change my life but how much
can a life be changed?'

'Aren't you scared what they'll say about you?'

'They'll say she speaks like an educated woman twice her
age and act surprised I'm not some gibbering wacko. They'll
say we didn't get to see her face because she is physically
scarred. They'll say I showed no emotion and that I was
calculating. That I was cold and that I'm a victim because I
won't dish the dirt on Thurman. But I'm not a victim; I'm
a survivor. I just don't want people to misunderstand him.'

Bob sets her jaw, squinting, measuring her somehow, then
smiles sadly.

'I feel like I've already had three lives: before Thurman;
with Thurman; and now. Now? Now I feel trapped inside

myself. They took more than his life with that bullet, they took me with him. I might have escaped but I don't know who I am, who I'm supposed to be.' She wants to keep talking forever, to say the unsayable and be damned if it upsets Bob.

'You sure you're ready for this?'

'Ready to stop all the bullshit, yeah. Tabloid insults and lies. Is it like essential you have to be a complete asshole to be a journalist? The things they've said. They's treating me worse than they treated Ingrid. Just 'cos I won't talk. You'll make sure no one gets a picture of me?'

'One hundred percent.'

The waitress appears. 'Want me to wrap that up?'

'No, thanks.'

'You like dessert?'

'Sure do,' Zoë says.

Bob watches her walk away.

'I thought I'd do the tour,' Zoë says. 'Of Coyote Plains.'

'No.'

'I can't. Course I can't. But . . .' A tone of risk.

Bob smiles, like she was expecting this. 'Am I about to be asked to do something that will compromise my career?'

Zoë reaches across the table and squeezes Bob's hand. 'I need to see the place one last time. It's where I grew up.' Daring Bob to interpret the look in her eyes. 'Thurman's watching over me. I can still sense him, and it makes me . . . Like the way he could touch me at times and make me feel so safe even though I knew that it was wrong. I loved a man who didn't deserve my love. I got to say goodbye. Properly.'

Bob scratches her neck, trying to hide whatever's running

through her mind. After a moment she says, 'They still setting things up. The fields and mining camps, I mean. They take a while to get established. The camp ain't anywhere near the ranch anyways, it's right out on the edge of the property. I know because they bought my friend's place the other side of the highway and I seen it with my own eyes. I doubt they got security down at the house, but even so . . .'

'Will you? Please.'

When Zoë gets back to the hotel she crosses the courtyard to where the birdcage hangs. She scans the windows; no one is peering out.

She opens the door to the cage.

'Go on. Fly. Be free.'

But the bird just sits there, blinking at her like she's dumb.

THEY DRIVE out of the city, heading west along a highway lined with scraggly prickly pear and creosote. The rockless, no-colored dirt, dry and desolate, turns flesh-pink in the fierce sunset, filling the interior of the jeep with blood-colored light. It drips off the clouds, spreading horizon-wide, sundown so rapid. They have been traveling for an hour to the soundtrack of Bob's CDs and the jeep's fat engine noise. Zoë requested the music but she is struggling with the tumbling thoughts in her head and has been talking non-stop. At times there is an excited babble between them both and they interrupt each other and finish each other's sentences, their faces lit brightly in each other's gaze.

This is Zoë's road movie. She pictures two actresses playing their parts and mimicking their dialogue, interior close-ups followed by a long shot of the jeep speeding towards the distant sketch of old, worn-down mountains.

She lowers the window and shoves her nose into the rustling wind. Closing her eyes, she inhales the air, faintly scented with greasewood and sage, reminding her of Thurman's body odor. She bites her nails and spits the tiny lunes out of the window.

Bob pulls into a lonely gas station and fills the tank, returning with candy and fizzy drinks and cans of iced tea. They drive another twenty miles into nowhere before turning off the blacktop onto a dust road, jouncing along a rutted track, the tires creating a Doppler effect that hurts Zoë's ears. The beams of the headlights stripe the flat table-country and studded scrubland that tell her she's home.

'We can stop and go back if you want?'

'You sure you know where you going?'

Bob turns to her, smiles. 'Trust me. What's in your bag?'

'Just something I need to leave behind.'

She sees the battered sails of the bore-hole lit in the jeep's headlights and again it is like she is experiencing the place in a movie, the movie of her eight years at Coyote Plains, and it all comes back to her: the pain and blood of the miscarriage; being hooked by the cacti; tumbleweed being tossed into the air by the chopper's rotor-wash; calling for Thurman in the desert-dark, thinking she was heading back to him, to make peace and start over. Though it feels like she has stepped out of scene.

Bob cuts the engine and hits the dome light.

Zoë holds out her trembling hands, stares at them.

'I'm right here. It looks like there's no one around, but you better use this, just in case.' Bob passes a heavy flash-light. 'He's gone, you know. There ain't nothing to be afraid of in there. Nothing. It's just an empty house, that's all.'

'No, it's not,' Zoë says. 'It's my home.'

She stands on the veranda playing the flashlight around the colored pieces of card with numbers on; next to the hole in the screen door, the number 12. She recalls the fine mist of blood that hung in the air after she shot the dogs, the beauty of that perfect moment. She walks through the hallway, footfalls synchronized with her heart-beat, and enters the kitchen. Across the wooden floor are the tracks of the many shoes that have stepped through the dust; dust from the desert outside, but also from the skin of tourists and mine employees. Strangers touching her things.

She spots the coils of her hair on the floor next to the sink.

She walks over to the table where a thick coating of mica glitters across the oilcloth, dotted with the spalls of dead insects, and thinks about all the cleaning she did over the years. A total waste of time. Her eyes follow the circle of light over the wood-burning stove and wicker furniture and enormous mantel clock, its hands stuck at 2:30. She points the beam towards the ceiling, at the meat hooks hanging down. Bob was right, nothing has been moved. It is exactly as she remembers it, apart from all the dust and numbers everywhere.

She calls into the silence of the house, 'Thurman?'

The linger of him, seeping through her.

In the parlor one of his manuals lays open, face down on the arm of his chair. She walks over to the old portable Victrola and finds a record on the turntable Townes Van Zandt. She lays the flashlight next to the Victrola, takes the heavy bag from her shoulder and rubs the dust from the record. She turns it on at the plug and then lifts the needle and drops it into a groove. Scratchy music fills the room, mournful strings.

She steps into the darkness, opening her arms in that remembered moment of bliss when she was walking past him and he grabbed her, pulling her into the reassuring smell of his muscular chest. He began slow-dancing, and as she moved in time with him she sensed the blood whirling within them both, heightened and hot, the physical tension of his muscle and bone and sinew enveloping her, like he not only wanted to possess and erase her but to wear her skin and breathe her breaths and think her thoughts. Like he understood the mystery of living within her skin. His hands on her ass, she parted her legs, her pubic bone tight against his thigh as he steered her to the music. She never wanted that moment to end.

Feet kicking up dust, Zoë embraces darkness, emptiness.

It feels like she is bleeding inside.

She was with him every day for eight years and can't believe she won't see or feel him anymore. There is no such thing as moving on. What happened to her will travel with her and that means carrying her past. In this way he isn't dead.

She is no longer Zoë Nielsen. All that's left of Zoë is scar tissue.

She is the dream of Thurman Hayes.

She picks up the bag and heads through the garage, music growing distant behind her. Her breath becomes shallow as she descends the tight passageway, treading between numbers, the twenty-five steps she always used to count. She can still smell the mold climbing the walls but can't smell the reek of herself anymore. The passageway is smaller than she remembers and when she reaches the bottom step she can go no further. She shines the flashlight towards the wall and sees how he chipped his way out around the door handle.

'Thurman.'

She removes the cans of lighter fluid from her shoulder bag.

Bob's fingers thread into hers, voice soft but urgent, 'We need to go.'

Zoë looks down into the dirt where her footprints lead back towards the burning ranch house and she knows in an instant that those are the impressions of Ingrid's feet. She looks ahead, squinching her eyes into the flickering light, and sees a figure walking in the flames.

'Ingrid?'

She watches her earthly shadow, the ghost of her former self fitting her feet into Ingrid's footprints and following the tracks back towards the flames, and she knows that when she gets there Ingrid will have unfurled a blanket on the sand and it will be the hottest day of the year. They will lie side by side, touching hands, smiling up into the sunshine, into a heat that melts the mind.

A young, nameless woman takes a step back into darkness, and begins the journey to leave herself behind.